Come Home to Little House
Five Generations of Pioneer Girls

WHERE LITT
Martha Morse
Laura's great-gra
born 1782

D0395211

BOSTON'S LITTLE HOUSE GIRL
Charlotte Tucker
Laura's grandmother
born 1809

SPIRIT OF THE WESTERN FRONTIER
Caroline Quiner
Laura's mother
born 1839

AMERICA'S ORIGINAL PIONEER GIRL
Laura Ingalls
born 1867

PIONEER FOR A NEW CENTURY
Rose Wilder
Laura's daughter
born 1886

The Little House

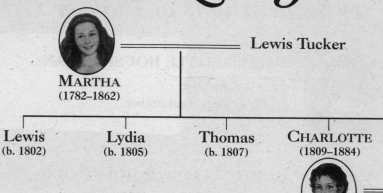

MARTHA
(1782–1862)

Lewis Tucker

Lewis
(b. 1802)

Lydia
(b. 1805)

Thomas
(b. 1807)

CHARLOTTE
(1809–1884)

Joseph
(1834–1862)

Henry
(1835–1882)

Martha
(1837–1927)

Mary
(1865–1928)

LAURA
(1867–1957)

Family Tree &

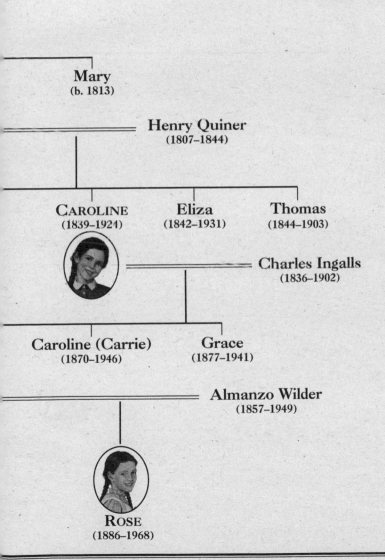

Mary
(b. 1813)

Henry Quiner
(1807–1844)

CAROLINE
(1839–1924)

Eliza
(1842–1931)

Thomas
(1844–1903)

Charles Ingalls
(1836–1902)

Caroline (Carrie)
(1870–1946)

Grace
(1877–1941)

Almanzo Wilder
(1857–1949)

ROSE
(1886–1968)

On the Other Side of the Hill

Roger Lea MacBride

Illustrated by David Gilleece

HarperTrophy®
A Division of HarperCollinsPublishers

On the Other Side of the Hill
Text copyright © 1995 by the Estate of Roger Lea MacBride
Illustrations copyright © 1995 by David Gilleece

Library of Congress Cataloging-in-Publication Data
MacBride, Roger Lea, 1929–1995
    On the other side of the hill / Roger Lea MacBride ; illustrated by David
Gilleece
        p.   cm.
    Summary: In the early 1900s, young Rose Wilder and her parents
struggle with a series of natural disasters on their farm in Missouri.
    ISBN 0-06-024967-6. — ISBN 0-06-024968-4 (lib. bdg.)
    ISBN 0-06-440575-3 (pbk.)
    1. Wilder, Laura Ingalls, 1867–1957—Juvenile fiction.   [1.Wilder, Laura
Ingalls, 1867–1957—Fiction.   2. Frontier and pioneer life—Missouri—
Fiction.   3. Farm life—Missouri—Fiction.   4. Missouri—Fiction.]
I. Gilleece, David, ill.   II. Title.
PZ7.M4782750n   1995   95-14263
[Fic]—dc20   CIP
                                                                     AC

❖

To my sisters Patricia and Pamela,
whom I called Pots and Pans when we were
all younger than Rose in this book.
Never mind what they called me!

Contents

On the Other Side of the Hill

Shivaree

In the inky blackness just behind Rose Wilder, a foot stepped on a twig with a loud crack. She jammed her fingers in her ears, and her whole body cringed as she waited for the shotgun to bark and spit its tongue of fire. All around her, in the soft glow of turned-down lanterns, stirred the ghostly shadows of well-wishers from Abe and Effie's wedding.

But the explosion did not come. Rose heard only the faint whispers of the people, the soft endless chirping of crickets, and the fluttering of a bird startled from its sleep. A cool late-summer breeze sighed through the leaves, and a limb groaned a small complaint.

A little way off in a clearing, Rose could just make out the small log house. Its dark windows looked blankly out on the forest. No smoke curled from its chimney. Curing raccoon and rabbit pelts covered the walls, their legs spread as if hugging the logs.

That was the house where Abe and Effie were beginning their new life together. Tonight their friends and kinfolk were going to give them a proper housewarming.

Abe Baird was the hired hand who helped Papa with his chores. Effie Stubbins was a big sister of Rose's best friend, Alva. The Stubbinses lived just a little way up Fry Creek from Rocky Ridge Farm, where Rose and her Mama and Papa had come to live two years ago from South Dakota. They had come here to Missouri to start a new life in the Ozark Mountains.

Abe and Effie had been married this very night. After the wedding, and after a wonderful feast and hours of dancing in one of Mr. Stubbins' barns, Abe and Effie had ridden off to the little log house in the new wagon Mr. Stubbins had given them for a present. He had even given them their own team of matched bay mules to pull it.

Now the crowd of Abe and Effie's friends and family waited in the darkened forest to shivaree the new couple. Papa was there, too. Mama had gone home to rest after dancing almost every tune with Papa. "I can scarcely keep my eyes open," she'd said through a big yawn. "You go on without me."

"What's shivaree?" Rose had asked Alva as they helped Mrs. Stubbins dry the feast dishes in the kitchen.

"I ain't sure," Alva had said, brushing a strand of red hair from her face with the back of a wet hand. Her red ribbons had gotten lost in the dancing, and her braids had come undone. Rose and Alva had danced all night, too, although it was more jumping and stomping than dancing.

"I ain't never done no shivareeing," said Alva. "My papa says it's kindly a ruckus-making in the dark of night, like they do on Christmas.

It's to wake up and serenade them that's just got married, to bring 'em good luck."

"It's a plain passel of noise and fun," Mrs. Stubbins had said with a chuckle. "Mind that platter, Alva, or you'll chip it. I recollect the night me and Mr. Stubbins was shivareed. You never heared such a carrying-on as that."

When all the dishes had been dried and put away in the china safe, Mr. Stubbins had gathered the wedding party in his stock barn. As the curious horses peered with shining eyes through the stall rails, he handed out old pots and pans, some tin horns, and cowbells. Two men put a big stick through the hole in the middle of a round saw-blade to carry it.

Swiney, Abe's little brother, who was eight years old, picked a cowbell; and Alva, who was nine, the same age as Rose, took two rusty railroad spikes to clink together.

Last, Mr. Stubbins brought out a drum. At least Rose thought it looked like a drum. It was an empty molasses keg with a groundhog skin stretched over one end, and the other end open. But in the middle of the skin was a hole

4

with a long string through it, and a button on the end of that string.

"What is it?" Rose wanted to know.

"This here's a dumb bull," Mr. Stubbins said, "and it makes a racket that'll put the hair up on top of your head."

Rose laughed and touched the top of her head. She couldn't wait to hear it. Would her hair really stand up? Would it look like a rooster's crown?

When everyone had picked a noisemaker, they set out, some in wagons and others following on foot, down the dark road under the setting moon. Abe's little sharecropper's cabin sat on twenty acres of land that Rose's papa and mama had just bought from another family. That family had given up farming in the Ozarks because it was too hard. They had moved away.

Now Abe and Effie were going to live on Rocky Ridge Farm, not very far from the little house where Rose lived with Papa and Mama.

Rose had loved Abe almost from the moment she met him, after he had come to apologize when Papa caught his little brother Swiney stealing eggs from Mama's henhouse. Abe played the fiddle and told wonderful stories about olden days in the Ozarks.

Abe was just a young man, and Swiney was a wild little boy in shabby clothes. Their mother and father had died, and they were alone in the world with hardly enough to eat.

But now Abe worked with Papa on the farm, helping with the crops, timbering trees into fence rails and railroad cross-ties. Mama had gentled Swiney some with proper clothes, good food, and even teaching him his lessons.

Now that Abe and Effie were married, they would all live and work and play together on Rocky Ridge, just like family. It was a wonderful cozy feeling for Rose. She was an only child, and all her other family, Grandma and Grandpa Ingalls and all her aunts, still lived in South Dakota. Before Abe and Swiney had come to Rocky Ridge, Rose had used to get so lonesome.

Now the shivaree party had snuck up close to Abe and Effie's house. One by one, the lanterns guttered and went out, cloaking the woods in full darkness. In her left hand Rose held the rusty tin pot that Mr. Stubbins had given her. Her other hand held a stout stick to beat it with. She hugged herself against the night chill.

"Why doesn't it start?" Rose whispered impatiently to the pale smudge of Alva's face.

"Hush, now!" a voice scolded nearby.

Then came a roaring sound like nothing Rose had ever heard, like some wild, angry beast; like a mad, pawing, raging bull. It went on and on, rising and falling, moaning and wailing; a horrible sound that made her legs tingle and her scalp crawl, and put her hair up on top.

Everywhere around her people were sniggering and guffawing. Then she spied Mr. Stubbins in the pale moonlight, pulling on the string, pulling it through the skin on that keg, on the dumb bull. It was the string rubbing against the hide that made that awful noise.

Just then the forest flashed bright for an instant and the air shattered with a great *BOOM!* from the shotgun. Rose flinched and dropped her stick. The deafening roar echoed through the hills.

The whole crowd surged forward, shouting and beating on pots and pans, tooting their horns, ringing their cowbells, the dumb bull roaring above it all. The men carrying the big round saw-blade held it up off the ground while a third man struck it with a hammer, *GONG! GONG! GONG!*

Rose picked up her stick and beat the little tin pot with all her might. The crashing noises so filled her ears that her own voice, laughing and shouting, sounded small and far away: "Shivaree! Shivaree! Abe 'n' Effie! Shivaree!"

In an instant the crowd had surrounded the house. Some boys climbed a tall tree and lit firecrackers that they threw to the ground, exploding with a flash and a bang. The air trembled with clanking and ringing and roaring and clocking and gonging and clanging and *BOOM!*— another blinding blast from the shotgun. Rose shrieked with delight. Her whole body trembled.

"I bet they could hear it all the way to town!" Alva shouted.

Then, in one of the windows of the log house, a shy glimmer of pale light winked. That made everyone beat harder and shout louder.

"Abimelech Noah Baird!" Mr. Stubbins' big voice boomed out, calling Abe by his whole name. "You'uns best show your faces. I cain't hold the folks back nary minute longer!"

Now in the window showed the brighter flare of a lamp being lit. The light flowed out of that window into the kitchen window. The crowd surged toward the front door just as it swung open with a loud creak.

Abe stepped out, a big, shy grin on his smooth face, his thick black hair tousled every which way, his overalls thrown on in such a rush that one of the galluses had slipped off his shoulder. Now all the lamps were turned up, and the clearing shimmered with light.

Rose scrunched between Papa and Mr. Stubbins to see better.

Abe held the lantern up high and squinted at the faces in the crowd. Then he threw his head back and roared with laughter. Effie's small face peered out from behind Abe's shoulder, her hands to her cheeks, her eyes big and round and dark. She looked as neat and trim as if she had just stepped out of a Sunday morning church service, her long blond hair tucked up in a bun. ·

After a fresh gust of clanging and laughter and hooting, the crowd quieted.

"I quit a-waiting on you'uns," Abe said heartily. "A-reckoned you folks was a-feeling puny and the shivaree were put off for 'nother night. We went to sleep. You tricked us after all!"

"Wouldn't be a right proper weddin' without there was a shiv'ree!" a man cried out. "It'd be bad luck!"

"That's right, son," declared Mr. Stubbins. "Now step on over and get your medicine like a big man or you ain't fitten for my daughter's hand."

"Oh, Papa!" Effie cried out. "You're a-shaming me afore all the folks." But then she giggled.

Abe glanced at Effie and smiled. Then he shambled into the yard, hands jammed into his pockets. The crowd parted like water around a rock. Two men stepped forward carrying a fence rail from each end.

Abe had been to a shivaree before, so he knew just what to do. He straddled the thin rail and sat down on it with a wince.

"This thing's right comfy," he joked. "Beats my bony old mule by a country mile."

Then the two men carried him bouncing all around the house while everyone cheered and followed and took up the racket again. Rose and Alva skipped behind, beating their noisemakers.

Effie stayed in the doorway, her hands covering her mouth, giggling crazily.

But on the third trip around the house, the fence rail split with a loud crack, dumping poor Abe on the ground like an old rag doll. Everyone fell silent, in shock.

"Oh, no!" an old woman cried out. "Hit's a bad omen!"

Abe stood up, shook his legs out, and brushed off the dirt.

"Now, don't you be a-worrying the poor boy

on his weddin' night," chided Mr. Stubbins.

"Hit's a bad omen," the woman declared in a shrilling voice. "I seen hit afore. Hit breaks the luck, the rail a-splitting so."

"Shut your mouth, Ora Bea!" a man's voice answered her. "Keep your nose to yourself and ain't nobody a-going to cut it off."

A murmur of approval rippled through the crowd and the old woman kept her mouth shut. But everyone shifted uneasily, waiting. In the darkness beyond, a horse nickered. Here and there Rose heard the soft *ding* of a bell or a pot shifting in someone's hand. But no one took up the shivaree again.

Finally Abe chuckled. "Well, shucks!" he boomed out. "Let's get on with it. Effie! Bring the bowl!"

Effie, her eyes sparkling, giggling and flushed, brought a big bowl of stick candy and nuts. Everyone took something to eat. Then Abe went into the house and brought out a box of cigars. Swiney snatched one when Abe wasn't looking, but Papa made him give it back.

Then Abe handed one to each of the men and soon the air was full of friendly chatter and strong tobacco smoke.

Finally, the candy was gone and everyone was yawning. Family by family they called out—"Good night!" "Good luck!" "Congratulations!"—and drifted off to their wagons and homes, swallowed up by the dark forest. Lantern lights bobbed and twinkled through the trees, and every so often a *clank* of a pot drifted back, followed by a burst of laughter.

The great day was ended.

Three's Company

Papa took Rose's hand so she wouldn't stumble over roots and stones.

"Moon's set already," he said through a big yawn. "We best get on home. It'll be morning soon enough and time to start the chores. Where's that little sprout?" Then Papa spied Swiney standing near Abe and Effie. Abe shook hands with the last of the shivaree-ers.

"Come along, son," Papa called out. "You'll stay with us tonight."

Swiney, his rumpled shirt pulled all out of his trousers and a smear of pot soot on his cheek, looked at Papa in surprise. "What for?" he demanded.

Papa walked over and put a hand on Swiney's shoulder. "I'd say three's a crowd, wouldn't you?"

Swiney edged away, his eyebrows pinched in suspicion.

"I ain't no crowd," he declared. "Abe's kin, and there's plenty room here for us three. Ain't that so, Abe?" He looked up at Abe with pleading eyes. But Abe just looked at Papa with a helpless shrug.

Papa's mustache twitched a little, and a tiny smile flitted across his lips.

Rose was nearly as confused as Swiney. But she knew Papa wouldn't say such a thing, Three's a crowd, if it wasn't so.

"Now, it's just for a day or two," Papa said in the soothing voice he used to calm a skittish horse. "Just 'til Abe and Effie get themselves settled; 'til they get used to things being new. You understand, don't you, son?"

Swiney scowled and shot a hard glance at Effie.

"Sonny boy, don't be a-getting feisty," Abe

said in his deep, throaty voice. "Mr. Wilder's got it all right. You go along with him now. I'll be a-coming by in the morning to start the haying, and we can let Effie go to her housekeeping in peace."

Swiney stood stock-still, rooted as a tree stump.

"Go on, now," Abe coaxed.

Swiney kicked at a stick on the ground. Then his shoulders sagged. He stuck his hands in his pockets and stalked off into the darkness beyond the circle of Papa's lantern. Papa and Rose fell in behind. Rose could hear Swiney muttering crossly under his breath, and the *crack* of a stick he was using to hit tree trunks.

"Papa, what is a bad omen?"

"An omen is a sign," he said, turning up the lantern wick so they could see their way better. "Some folks think signs can tell the future, if it'll be good or bad. Omens are as old as humankind and not much in fashion these days. But a lot of folks here in the Ozarks still believe in 'em."

"Is it an omen to plant potatoes in the old of

the moon?" Rose wondered. Mama always planted underground crops—potatoes, turnips, radishes, and onions—after the full moon was past, and aboveground crops like cabbage and tomatoes when the moon was new.

"That's different," Papa said. "An omen is something unexpected. Seeing a black cat is supposed to be an omen of bad luck. An old farmer in town once told me that if you step on a toad, your cows'll give spoiled milk. But those are just old superstitions. They can't be true."

"What about the fence rail breaking, like that woman said?" Rose asked, hopping over a log that blocked their path. Somewhere nearby a screech owl cried out mournfully, and Rose stopped for an instant, listening. "Is it really a bad omen? Will bad luck come to Abe and Effie?"

Papa chuckled. "I can't see what an old broken rail has to do with bad luck, except now Abe must cut a new one. Don't you fret about omens, Rose. Worrying is like sitting in a rocking chair. It gives you something to do, but it never gets you anyplace."

Swiney kept to himself all the way home, and barely said a word as Mama made up a pallet for him to sleep on in Rose's new attic room. Rose was very tired when she carefully hung up her good dress on the rope in the corner and wriggled into her nightgown. She yawned twice saying her prayers, and blew out the lamp. Then she climbed into the new grown-up bed that Papa had made for her. The tick stuffed with straw crunched cozily as she snuggled down.

The memories of that day were a store for Rose's mind to dwell on. Abe and Effie's new home had been dedicated in a proper and fitting manner. Rose could imagine Effie standing by Abe through thick and thin, fighting for him like a determined bird defending its nest.

"G'night, Swiney," she said to the darkness.

"G'night," Swiney softly answered.

Rose began drifting off almost as soon as her head touched the pillow.

"Rose?" Swiney whispered loudly. "You awake?"

"Mmmm."

Rose listened to the little night noises, wait-ing. From the barn she heard one of the horses nicker softly. "What?" she finally asked.

"You reckon Abe's a-going to 'low me to come back? I mean, to stay with him and Effie?"

"Of course," said Rose. "He's your family. Now Effie is, too."

"I dunno," Swiney muttered. Rose heard him stir restlessly in his covers. "What if Effie don't want me to? Maybe she won't."

"Of course she will. Don't worry, Swiney. Abe said it's just for a day or two."

Swiney was quiet again. Rose pulled the covers tighter around her and snuggled her bottom into a hollow place between two lumps in the tick. The straw had gotten mashed hard, and she reminded herself to unbutton the tick and stir it up in the morning to make it soft again.

"Rose?"

"What?" Rose said a bit more peevishly than she meant.

"You sure are lucky."

"I am?" she asked in surprise.

"You got yourself a real mama and a real papa. They could never put you out, not for nothing. I wish they was my mama and papa. I wish Abe hadn't of married Effie. Then everything could be the same."

Rose lay still, staring into the darkness, not knowing what to say. Her thoughts began to wake her up. Swiney had no mother and father, no little brothers and sisters to play and grow up with him.

But Rose had tried to be like a big sister. Mama and Papa had taken care of him almost as their own. And Effie was kindhearted. Rose knew she would never treat Swiney cruelly. It wasn't so bad, really, if only Swiney could see it that way.

She was about to tell him that when she heard the soft purring noise of his snoring.

Rose sighed. She *was* lucky, now she thought about it. And she wouldn't let any superstitious old woman worry her about bad omens. Everything was going to turn out just fine.

She closed her eyes and let herself drift

down and down toward sleep. The last thing she heard was the trembling wail of the screech owl, far away now, its lonesome voice fading in her ears.

I'm a Man!

Swiney slept two nights in Rose's room. She surprised herself by enjoying his company. After supper and after evening chores, they played checkers on a board Papa had made from a plank of hickory wood. He had carved lines in it to make the squares and stained half the squares dark brown with the hull of a walnut. He had carved the round checker pieces, too, staining half of them to match.

Mama popped a bowl of popcorn, and Rose and Swiney sat in front of the fireplace on the little rag rug eating between sips of their glasses of milk. Rose read aloud from one of Mama's books of poetry and from *Robinson Crusoe*, one of Rose's favorite books. Mama even let Blackfoot, the orange cat, come inside for a visit. She curled right up in Rose's lap, contentedly purring and licking her hand.

Swiney sat with his chin in his hands, listening with bright eyes that grew round as barrel lids when Rose read of Crusoe's adventures with lions and other wild beasts in Africa. He asked questions about the words he didn't know, and Rose patiently corrected his English. Swiney had never been to school. He swore he would never go. Even if he'd wanted to, the growing farm kept every spare hand busy from lamplight to lamplight.

Mama even kept Rose home from school at times to help with the chores. Rose didn't mind, except she missed her best school friend, Blanche Coday. The lessons bored her. She'd rather read a book by herself any time.

So Mama gave Rose her lessons at home, and when there was time, Swiney too. He still had trouble remembering to say "isn't" instead of "ain't." And he still tacked an "a" before some of his verbs, the way the Ozarks hill people did. But more and more he tried to speak properly. Rose was proud of the changes in Swiney since he had come into their lives.

During the days Rose and Swiney helped harvest the oats that Papa had planted in the new ground he'd bought from Mr. Kinnebrew. Papa had left many of the trees standing. It was too hard to dig out the roots. But he deadened the trees by cutting the bark off in a ring all the way around. That was called girdling. Girdling killed the tree so it wouldn't grow leaves. Then sunlight could reach the ground to grow the crops.

When they had first moved to Rocky Ridge Farm, nearly all of it had been in timber, and they had had only a one-room tumbledown log house to live in. But in two years, bit by bit, Papa and Abe had cleared enough forest for the precious apple orchard, for corn and oats, the garden, hay meadow, and even a patch of grazing pasture for the livestock.

During the winters, Papa and Abe felled

trees in the timber lot. Some of the wood had gone into the new barn their first fall in Missouri. Last spring some of it had gone to build the new house, with Rose's first room of her own. But most of it was hacked into cross-ties that Papa sold to the railroad, and fence rails and stove wood that Papa sold in town.

There were so many mouths to feed now: the two mossy-faced mules named Roy and Nellie; Papa's sleek Morgan mares, Pet and May; Mama's chickens; and just that spring they had gotten their very own milk cow, Bunting, and her calf, Spark. And now there were the two other mules that Mr. Stubbins had given Abe and Effie when they married.

Rose swelled with pride to think that all those animals, and both families—the Bairds and the Wilders—could live from the thin, stony soil of their little farm.

One morning after the bright sun had climbed into the sky and drunk up the morning dew, Papa shouldered his big, gangly grain cradle and they all walked to the oat field. Abe carried a cradle too, one he'd borrowed from

Mr. Stubbins. Rose and Swiney followed skipping along the path to a tune Abe sang in his full, throaty voice.

> *"Had a poke o' greens,*
> *And a mess o' nubbins,*
> *But I gave 'em all away,*
> *To marry Effie Stubbins.*

> *"Swing Effie Stubbins,*
> *Swing her ma,*
> *Ever'body bow,*
> *To please her pa."*

"Is that a real song?" Rose asked suspiciously.

"You bet, little girl," Abe said tucking a shock of glossy black hair under his hat. "Only it's got words I made up for it:

> *"Looked down the road,*
> *Effie was a-coming,*
> *Thought to myself,*
> *I'll kill myself a-running.*

I'm a Man!

"Swing Effie Stubbins,
Then to your taw,
Then to the gal
From Arkansas."

Abe's singing put Rose in a wonderful mood. The brilliant sun smiled down on the farm and all its abundance, and the earth smiled back. Her heart felt light as a cloud. When they reached the oat field a morning breeze was rippling and whispering through the tawny grass. Rose waded in, scaring up waves of grasshoppers that flew off on rattling wings to land farther on, plopping down with a sound like fat drops of rain landing in dust.

Abe and Papa began the cutting, side by side, at one end of the field. They cut a big swath all the way across, swinging the cradles like giant bony hands that scooped up the long stalks and heavy heads in their palms.

With each swing the cradle's sharp blade cut the stalks and neatly laid them in its long wooden fingers with all the oat heads together. Then Papa and Abe dropped the oats in bunches on the ground and swung again, cutting new bunches. When they got all the way to the other end of the field, they stopped to mop their brows and sharpen the cradle blades with the whetstone Papa kept in his pocket. Then they turned around and cut their way back.

Rose and Swiney followed, picking up the bunches, bundling and tying them up in the middle with lengths of straw, like the sash on a dress. When they had tied up ten bundles, they shocked them in a stack, the bundles leaning against each other so they wouldn't fall. That way the oats would cure properly in the warm dry sun. After they cured for a few weeks, a belching steam-powered threshing machine would come and separate the grain from the straw.

It was prickly, dusty work, but Rose thought nothing smelled quite so good as the sweet, fresh scent of new-cut crops. She chewed a stem and thought what a shame it was that straw didn't taste as wonderful as it smelled.

Fido, Rose's little black-and-tan terrier,

raced about the field hunting mice and rabbits, scaring up flocks of quail, and playing with Blackfoot, who liked to catch and eat grasshoppers. Blackfoot was almost like a dog, the way she followed people wherever they walked.

Fido was too short to see over the tall oat grass. So as he ran he would leap into the air, legs poised as gracefully as a carousel pony, and quickly twist his head to either side to see what he could see. After he dropped back into the grass, he ran some more, and jumped again. Rose never knew where in the field Fido would come popping up, like a fish leaping out of water.

It was two years since Rose had found Fido, starving and frightened near the campsite, when she first came to Missouri with Mama and Papa. She was just as proud of Fido as she was of Swiney. Rose liked to see how the best could come out of any creature, even a starving dog.

They stopped cutting and shocking often to drink from the fresh jugs of cold spring water Mama brought to them in between her baking, separating the milk, churning the butter, cooking dinner, and all the other chores of the farm that never would be finished.

Some of those chores were Rose's, but not during good cradling weather, when she stayed busy helping get the oats cut and off the ground. After the grain had been shocked, Papa and Abe went through the field and capped all the shocks. On top of each shock they put two bundles and spread them out, to make a roof that would keep the rain off. Then the oats would stay dry in the field until the threshers came.

"Weather's been so good this year, the oat heads came in heavy. And we made three cuttings of hay," Papa boasted one night at supper. "Won't have to buy any forage for the livestock this winter. Just shows what folks can do if they put their minds to it and their backs in it, with a bit of Providence, of course."

"The garden has done well, too," said Mama. She flicked her napkin at a fly that was worrying the platter of boiled cabbage and onions. "We'll have another good harvest of potatoes, with plenty to trade in town. Even with prices low, we ought to be able to settle up our bill at Reynolds' store and have something left over for spring planting."

Papa broke a biscuit in half to sop the last bit of gravy from his plate. His nails were rough and chipped and two of them still showed black where he'd hurt them moving a heavy stone during spring plowing.

The backs of his hands were brown and leathery from working all summer in the sun. His face was leathery brown, too, up to the line on his forehead where his hat always sat when he went outdoors. Above the line his forehead glowed pale as a grub worm, except for a red spot over his right eye. That was where a piece of wood he was chopping had flown up and hit him.

Rose noticed for the first time that there were flecks of gray in Papa's wavy brown hair and in his mustache, like powdered sugar. And his hair was thinning in front, like the cut-over meadow. She tried to imagine Papa without any hair at all, but she couldn't.

Rose thought Mama looked as young and beautiful as ever, although her hands were rough and red from doing out a wash that day with the harsh lye soap. But her roan-colored hair was still long and shimmery in the lamplight. Her violet eyes still sparkled as she talked, pouring herself a fresh cup of tea from the pot.

Rose thought about how hard Mama and Papa worked, how they had worked hard all their lives, trying to make a life from the stubborn, grudging earth.

"If we can just make a couple more good years like this one," Mama said, "and then the apple trees come into bearing, we ought to be able to pay off the mortgage on this place, as well as the extra twenty acres we bought from Mr. Kinnebrew.

"For the first time since we moved here from South Dakota, I'm beginning to think all the work and drudgery of farming may be worth it after all."

"There's gold in a farm," Papa said, quoting the old saying that Rose had heard him say a hundred times before. So she quickly finished it before he could: "You just have to dig it out." Papa chuckled.

Just then Fido whined and whimpered from the porch, in the voice he used for greeting friends.

"I wonder who that could be?" Mama said, touching her hair. She fumbled with her apron strings, but before she could get them untied and open the door, the latchstring jiggled and tugged, and it swung open. Swiney stood there, a frown on his face.

"What is it, son?" Papa asked, pushing his chair back. "Step in, boy. Did you eat yet?"

Swiney shuffled into the kitchen and took off his straw hat. But he just stood there, clutching the limp, soiled brim and staring at the floor.

"Swiney, what's the matter?" Mama cajoled.

"It's Effie, Missus Wilder," he said, his voice catching piteously. "She throwed me out."

"Throwed you . . ." Mama chuckled at herself. "I mean, *threw* you out?" She cast a sidelong glance at Papa. "I can scarcely believe it. There must be some mistake."

Swiney plunked himself down in the extra chair by the cookstove and looked at Mama hopefully. "Can I stay by you'uns again, tonight?"

"Let me give you something to eat," Mama said. She fetched a plate from the china safe and uncovered the apple pie to cut a piece.

"Of course you can stay, if you need to," Papa said. "But let's hear the story first. What happened?"

So Swiney explained, tears lapping at the edge of his voice. The words tumbled out so fast that Rose could not understand at first what he was saying. Effie had told him to help her wash and dry the dishes, and she told him he had to sweep the floor, and to make up his own bed, and scrape his shoes before he came inside.

"She's a-bossing me around like I was a old mule, and . . . and . . . she says I got to help on wash day, too. But I ain't . . . er . . . I told her. I'm not never a-doing no girl's work." He spit the words out bitterly. Then his face went hard. "It ain't right, Mr. Wilder," he declared

34

in his boy's piping-high voice. "I'm a man!"

Mama turned her face toward the stove. Rose bit her lip hard and stared into her lap, picking at the folds of her apron. Swiney was a long way from being a man, but she wouldn't embarrass him by laughing out loud.

"Mmmmm," Papa said thoughtfully. He cleared his throat, pulled out his pipe, and slowly filled the bowl with tobacco from his leather pouch.

Mama set the plate of apple pie on the table.

"Eat up," she said gently. "It'll make you feel better." Swiney pulled his chair over and took a forkful. Rose got up to start clearing the dishes and covering the leftovers with clean cloths.

Papa lit his pipe, blew out a big cloud of spicy smoke, and leaned back in his chair. "Now, you say Effie threw you out of the house," he said.

Swiney's mouth was full of apple pie, so he only nodded his head.

"Seems to me Abe must have had something to say about it," said Papa. "I can't think that Effie would just throw you out."

"Abe says I got to mind Effie 'cause she's the boss of the house now. And Effie said if I don't like the rules, I could just git," Swiney said, wiping a bit of pie from the corner of his mouth. "So I gitted."

"You got," Mama corrected. "I mean, you went. Oh, you mix me up sometimes!" she exclaimed. "But I'm sure she was mostly teasing. Even so, if you were my boy you'd be helping with chores and I wouldn't cotton a fuss over it."

"But Missus Wilder," Swiney complained, "iffen folks seen me a-washing dishes and a-scrubbing sheets, they'd laugh and call me names. I want to go out with Abe and do man's work." Then he sighed heavily and buried his head in his hands. "Oh, why do I always get the worst of it?"

Rose dipped hot water from the reservoir of the cookstove into the washbasin. She dabbed the dishrag in the crock of soft soap and began to scrub the dishes clean. She was thinking all the time.

She knew Swiney wasn't work-lazy. He

helped Papa and Abe all he could. He even asked for work sometimes. He gathered brush in the woodlot, or hoed corn, or cut sprouts. Sometimes he got distracted by a rabbit, or stopped to throw stones at a snake or a wasp nest. But he worked hard the rest of the time.

Rose thought maybe it was a bit unfair of Effie to make Swiney do housework. That *was* a girl's job, after all. But Effie was all alone in her housekeeping. She probably needed some help now and then to keep up.

Suddenly Rose had a wonderful idea. It was so wonderful she blurted it right out. "I'll do it!" she cried.

Mama, Papa, and Swiney all turned to stare at her in surprise.

"What?" Mama said. "You'll do what?"

"I'll help Effie," Rose said. "I mean, we could all do our washing together, Mama. And I can help her with baking, or cleaning house, or beating rugs."

"That's swell, Rose!" Swiney shouted.

"But who will help me care for the chickens, and fetch wood for the stove, and water the livestock?" said Mama. "I can't spare you for those chores. You know we barely keep ahead as it is."

"Swiney could do them," Rose said. "He can come here in the morning and do my chores, and I can go and help Effie with hers."

Rose liked Effie, and of course she liked Abe. She thought it might be fun to help Effie set up housekeeping, and to help cook for Abe. And it would be something different from the same chores she did every day at home.

"I don't know," Mama said doubtfully, brushing the last crumbs off the table into the dishrag. "We have our hands full here as it is."

"Please, Missus Wilder," Swiney begged. "I'll work hard, I promise."

Papa got up, lifted one of the stove caps and tapped his pipe ashes into the coals. "You know, Bess, Rose has an idea. So long as the work gets done, maybe we ought to let the children sort it out."

Sneeze on Monday

Papa walked Swiney back to Abe and Effie's that night.

"No sense worrying your big brother about where you've run off to," he said.

Papa got back just as Rose was about to go to bed. She stood in her flannel union suit warming herself by the kitchen stove while Papa sat on a chair pulling off his boots. Mama was stirring the fire in the fireplace in the bedroom and putting on fresh logs for the night.

"Effie thought that was a fine idea you had, Rose," he said, grunting. "Here, give a pull on this one. It's stuck."

Rose sat on the floor and tugged on Papa's boot heel while he wiggled his foot loose. Finally it popped out, and he sighed with relief.

"For now, unless Mama needs you here, you can go to Abe and Effie's after breakfast and see if she needs any help. And Swiney will come here and help with our morning chores."

"*After* the breakfast dishes are done," Mama called out from the bedroom.

"Yes, Mama," Rose answered politely. But inside she was jumping for joy.

Now began the dry, dusty weeks just before harvest time when every living thing strained to finish its work before the first frost could come and kill it. Each day dawned crisp and clear. In the first light of the morning Rose found multitudes of spiderwebs in the grass and trees, jeweled with drops of dew. A yellow-striped garden spider sat in the middle of each one waiting for a meal to fall into its trap. By midmorning a purple haze fell over the hilltops. There was a hint of sadness in the sunshine.

In the gorge by the spring the big green walnuts began to drop. When Mama sent Rose to collect a pailful, the squirrels were too busy hiding away their winter store to stop and scold.

In the summery afternoons the pale leaves of the trees dozed under a thin blanket of dust. The weeds along the creek and the road were gray with it. Dragonflies skimmed and whirled about, and thistledown drifted in the wind. Grasshoppers rattled away on their yellow-flashing wings. Crickets sang their mournful song among the low clumps of grass.

The deep green of the corn had faded to pale brown, and now the dead leaves rustled dryly in the wind. Pumpkins that Rose had helped plant along the edges of the corn patch swelled and their color deepened, flaring like bright flames at sunset. Overhead the first flights of honking geese soared south, looking for a safe place to rest for the night.

Most mornings Rose rode her stubborn donkey, Spookendyke, to Abe and Effie's and spent an hour or so with Effie. Rose saw right

41

away that Effie was a good housekeeper. She didn't need very much help to keep up her chores, but she liked the company.

"I ain't accustomed to being alone," she told Rose as she ironed one of Abe's shirts. Rose sat at the table watching her work, sipping a cup of tea. Effie was small, a tiny bit taller than Mama, but slender like a young girl. She *was* a young girl, after all.

She moved around the house as gracefully as a sure-footed deer. Effie was very pretty, too, with skin that seemed to glow from the inside and long blond hair that she let down when she was at home doing chores.

Rose felt very grown-up sitting in that house, sipping tea and listening to Effie talk. She wrapped her hands around the warm cup, just the way Mama did.

"Long as I can recollect, our house was full up with kids and kin, and the barn had a passel of livestock in it," Effie said. "There was always some creature a-being birthed." The little table she was ironing on creaked each time she pushed the iron forward, like a cricket slowed down by cold weather—*creak, creak, creak.*

"When Abe asked me to wed, I had nary thought of a-going to live in a house without no flock of young'uns underfeet. And Abe stables the mules up in one of Kinnebrew's old sheds, so we ain't even got no barn!" She chuckled.

"But just you watch," she added, looking at Rose with a glint in her eye. "We're a-going to have us a mess of young'uns one day."

Rose giggled and blushed. Girls didn't talk about having babies in polite company. But she realized that Effie didn't think of her as company. She was another girl, a friend! Rose basked in the glow of that feeling for a moment. Then she thought about babies to play with, and that really stirred up her heart.

The iron glided smooth and fast over the faded blue chambray. Then Effie dropped the cooling iron on the stove with a clatter and clamped the handle onto a freshly hot one. It took Effie only three irons to finish a shirt. Rose needed six to do one of Papa's shirts. Mama could do it in four.

Effie chattered away. Rose could hardly get a word in edgewise, even to ask what chores she might do.

"Do?" Effie said in surprise. She looked around the little log room, her lips pursed in thought. "Oh, you could carry out them stove ashes, if you've a mind to. But sit a spell. Ain't no hurry. After all, what's time to a hog?"

One day while Rose kneaded bread and Effie cut dough into biscuits, they talked about omens and signs. "Do you believe them?" Rose asked. "Do you think they're true?"

"I wouldn't know for all of 'em," Effie said as her quick hands carefully arranged the little circles of dough in a baking pan. "There's a mess of signs to know about. My mama sets quite a store by 'em. I recollect oncet she was a-drying the dishes and dropped the towel. She said, 'Better clean up this place. Looks like company's a-coming.' And sure enough, presently a drummer come a-riding up the road, a-peddling knives."

Rose flopped the heavy ball of dough over and dusted it with flour. She rubbed an itch on her nose with the back of her wrist. "A towel dropping made the drummer visit?" Rose asked doubtfully. "My Papa says omens are just superstitions."

"It's so, Rose," Effie said earnestly. "Your papa ain't from these parts. You got to be born in these hills to know the signs.

"Iffen the towel drops two times, a stranger's a-coming hungry. Iffen a fork drops, a man's a-coming. Iffen the grounds in your coffee cup are a-clinging high up the sides, it's a sign company's a-bringing good news."

Effie told Rose more omens: If two roosters fight, two young men will soon visit. If your nose itches on the left, a woman is coming to visit; on the right, a man. Rose tried to remember if her nose had itched on the right or the left.

"My mama taught me an old sneezing rhyme," Effie said as she crouched in front of the oven. She opened the door, stuck her hand inside, and counted under her breath, "One, two, three, four. . . ." When she got to nineteen, she jerked it out.

"Just right," she declared. "Iffen you can

stand to hold it past twenty, it needs more heat." Now she took the pan of pale biscuit dough, slid it onto the rack, and shut the oven door with a clank. She lifted one of the caps to stir the coals and threw in a few sticks of wood.

"Let's see if I can recollect that old ditty:

"Sneeze on Monday, sneeze for fun,
Sneeze on Tuesday, see someone,
Sneeze on Wednesday, get a letter,
Sneeze on Thursday, something better,
Sneeze on Friday, sneeze for sorrow,
Sneeze on Saturday, a beau comes tomorrow,
Sneeze on Sunday, trouble on Monday."

As Rose rode home through the woods on Spookendyke, her head swam with thoughts. She wanted to believe in omens, to know the future. But if she believed, she would have to be very careful. She would always have to be thinking and watching and fretting. Some omens could tell of a coming death, and Rose did not want to know about that.

"I would wonder that Effie wasn't pulling your leg, these Ozarkers are such tale-tellers," Mama said when Rose told her about the omens. She was outside in the yard, emptying the old bed ticks of their straw stuffings. The ticks needed to be washed and restuffed with clean straw. Rose helped Mama turn the ticks inside out and shake out the last of the dust and bits of stem. They even found the dried-up body of a little mouse.

"Omens and signs are superstitions left over from ancient times," Mama said, brushing dust from her hands. "They are a kind of old-fashioned entertainment for country people. You mustn't pay them any mind."

But Rose decided she would try harder to notice all the omens that Effie had told her about and see if they could be true. For many days she tried dropping the dish towel and a fork, and her nose itched a lot, on both sides. But no strangers came.

Cider Pressing

Now began the hurried weeks when all across the rolling hills each hand on every farm worked long days, even at night under the bright harvest moon, gathering in the crops. Rose woke in the darkness before dawn to the sound of rattling stove caps and the smell of coffee.

She lit her lamp with fingers stiff from the work of the day before. She hunched shivering as she threw on her everyday dress, then rushed downstairs to warm herself by the cookstove and help Mama with breakfast. She didn't even stop to brush her hair. The only thing any of them thought about was getting in the harvest in time.

The Bairds and the Wilders decided to eat together during the harvest, to save Effie the chore of cooking and cleaning up, so the work would go faster. Each morning, just as the first pale light of the new day showed itself beyond the apple orchard, Abe, Effie, and Swiney drove into the barnyard, their eyes still puffy with sleep. Swiney huddled between Abe and Effie, hugging himself against the morning chill. The mules breathed veils of steam that floated like tiny clouds in the still morning air.

Swiney and Abe helped Papa with the feeding and watering of the animals, and the milking. Mama, Effie, and Rose peeled potatoes or kneaded bread dough, rolled pie crusts, fried the meat, and stirred the beans. Then they all sat down to a big, hearty breakfast before rushing off to that day's work. The house chores got no more than a lick and a promise.

The potatoes were dug up, a wagonload was

sent to town, and the rest were buried in straw and earth for wintering over. The sweet potatoes were dug up, cleaned, carefully wrapped in bits of old newspaper, and set in a box in the kitchen.

The pole beans that grew up the cornstalks were cut and stored in feed sacks to dry in the barn. When the pods were dry, they would beat the sacks with sticks to hull the beans.

The last planting of cabbage was cut, and some of the heads were buried upside down in the earth, to keep them fresh a little while longer. One morning Rose and Effie sat at the kitchen table using sharp knives to finely shred the rest of the snowy heads.

Mama got out two molasses barrels and wetted the insides with vinegar. She poured a layer of salt in the bottoms and began to pack them tightly with the shredded cabbage. She added another layer of salt, and another of cabbage, until the barrels were packed full. The last thing she did was sprinkle a handful of juniper berries on top.

When Abe came in for dinner, Mama made

him stand on the barrelheads and jump up and down, to press the cabbage down even tighter. Mama set the barrels in a corner of the kitchen to let the cabbage ferment. When it was done, she would open the barrels, drain the liquor, and add fresh brine. Then they would have kraut to fry up with salt pork.

Before the first frost Papa brought back a wagonload of apples from Rippee's orchard. He ground-stored about half of them. Then began the long slow job of peeling and cutting up all the rest, and drying them in the sun on old sheets.

Rose, Mama, and Effie sat on the porch in their bonnets and bare feet all morning and all afternoon, peeling and slicing, peeling and slicing, and telling stories. All the time Rose worked, she ate apple slices, until Mama told her to stop or she'd make herself sick.

Mama sat in the rocking chair that Papa had made for her last Christmas and told a story about the time a panther chased her great-grandpa through the Big Woods of Wisconsin.

Effie told haint stories, about ghosts who

showed themselves in graveyards and in the windows of empty houses and could make doors slam. She told about the time her uncle Clabe visited Breadtray Mountain in Stone County and heard the sobs and groans of Spanish soldiers who had been killed there many, many years ago. Rose listened spellbound.

"Land sakes! What a gruesome story!" Mama said, setting a pailful of the bright-red peelings on the step for Swiney to feed to the chickens. "Rose, a bird's going to nest in your mouth if you don't close it. And mind you don't peel the skins so thick."

Rose gulped and bent to her work. She had never been in a haunted house, or visited a graveyard, or even heard a haint story. The thought of a person's soul wandering the earth frightening people sent delicious shivers up her spine.

When she wasn't cutting and peeling, it was Rose's job to protect the drying slices: shooing the flies, chasing away the greedy chickens, and watching for rain. When Rose spied a rain cloud coming on, they all rushed out and snatched up the sheets full of slices to bring into the house. When the sun returned, they spread the sheets and had to lay out all the slices again.

Finally one afternoon, when all the apples had been peeled and cut, the last sheetful was laid out to dry. Rose and Effie were busy stirring the slices so every side could get some sun, when Papa drove the wagon into the yard. He tied the horses' reins to a tree.

The sweaty flanks of the sleek Morgans, Pet and May, gleamed like polished wood. They stamped their feet, butted heads, and playfully nipped. Their friskiness told Rose they had just driven from town.

Papa liked to drive fast, and Pet and May liked to run. The mares had grown up on the flat, open South Dakota prairie, and even after two years they still missed racing the wind on the long smooth roads. The Ozark hills were steep. The roads were snaky and full of rocks and stumps to hurt their feet. The only place they could run was on the road out of town, which was not so bumpy.

Rose took pity on the mares and gave each a treat of dried apple. Then she stood on tiptoe to peer into the wagon-box. She gasped.

"Oh, Papa, no!" she groaned, slumping down against the wheel to sit on the ground.

The wagon was full of apples!

Rose would never cry over a load of apples, but her eyes burned anyway; she was so tired of peeling and slicing. Her right index finger was raw where she held the knife handle. The web of her left thumb stung from a deep cut. She had handled so many apples she had even dreamed of them. She couldn't, not for anything, peel one more apple.

"Don't be so quick to jump to your conclusions." Papa chuckled. "These aren't eating apples. They're culls, and we're taking them to the Stubbinses' for a cider pressing. Tell Mama to quick boil up some water and scald a barrel. See if you can't hunt up a couple of empty jugs, too."

Rose jumped to her feet and shouted with delight. A trip to the Stubbinses' was always an adventure, and it didn't sound like very much work. Of course, it was a chance to visit with Alva. Since the wedding, Rose had been too busy with her chores. And even though she'd peeled and sliced and dreamed a mountain of apples, a drink of cider sounded like just the ticket.

"Step along, now," Papa said. "I've got to clean out the mule stalls before we go. We'll have to hurry if we're to be back in time for evening chores. And after supper, if we can catch some moonlight, we'll start cutting and shocking the corn."

Rose raced inside the house. Mama stood on a chair, hanging a sack of dried apples from a rafter. Rose grabbed the bail of the cedar water bucket, but it slipped from her hand and clunked to the floor.

"Sakes alive, Rose!" Mama cried out. "You startled me. Where's the fire?"

Rose paced back and forth and swung the bucket impatiently as she gave Papa's message. Then she dashed out to fetch water from the spring.

———

Rose could smell the sweet scent of apples before she even jumped down from the wagon in the Stubbinses' barnyard. Papa climbed down while Mama held the reins. Then he guided the team backward until the wagon-box sat by the barn door.

Inside, in the hallway, baskets of apples lay everywhere in the straw. A group of grown-ups and excited children huddled like hungry bees around a tall machine with a big iron wheel on top. Several families had come that day to use Mr. Stubbins' press. In return, they would give Mr. Stubbins some of their cider.

The barn echoed with the high, light voices of children and the splash and gurgle of pouring cider. Rose took a deep breath of the winey air that was so thick it seemed to flow like water over the bare skin of her arms.

She finally spotted Alva sitting on a milking stool, surrounded by baskets of apples.

"Alva!" Rose shouted.

Alva looked up and grinned at Rose with her big snaggly-toothed smile. She pushed her bonnet back to see better.

"What are you doing?" Rose asked.

Alva had an apple in one hand and a paring knife in the other. "These here apples are the falls that was picked off the ground. I'm a-cutting out the ruint parts afore they get pomaced."

"I never saw a cider pressing before," Rose said, looking at the crowd around the machine. Everyone was sipping cider from a cup or a glass. "And I forgot to bring a cup."

Alva grabbed Rose's hand and pulled her across the straw-covered floor to the press. It was a wooden machine that stood on legs. Mr. Stubbins was dumping apples into a box on the top. Alva said that was the hopper.

Another man cranked a handle that turned a spiky metal wheel under the hopper that smashed up the apples as they came out. Then that wheel spat the smashed apples—the pomace—into a wooden barrel that had open spaces between the staves. That was the slat.

When the slat was full of pomace, the men slid it sideways under the press. They turned the big metal wheel on top, and that screwed

the round board of the press slowly down,
squashing the pomace. Juice began to pour
between the staves as the press smashed the
pomace flatter and flatter. The juice ran into a
chute and out a small hole into a bucket.

Alva fished in the pocket of her pinafore and
pulled out a tin cup. She quick stuck it in the
foamy brown waterfall of cider and caught a
cupful.

"Here," Alva said. "Have a drink."

Rose giggled and took the tin cup.

"What's so funny?" Alva demanded.

"I was thinking of the first time I saw you.
You tricked me into eating a puckery persimmon," Rose said, brushing away a bee that
kept diving at the cup. "It tasted horrible."

"You didn't know nothing about a-living in
the hills then," Alva said, her pale-blue eyes
lighting up with mischief. "You was an easy
trick. But you're a-getting right smart for me,
and we're friends now. The only thing in that
cup is good drinking cider."

Rose took a big, long gulp. The cider rolled
smooth and sweet over her thirsty tongue. It

went down her throat as cool and refreshing as spring water.

Rose let out a loud, "Ahhhhh," and then hic-cupped.

"C'mon." Alva laughed. "I got to finish them falls. We can talk whilst I'm a-cutting."

They remembered and laughed about the shivaree. Rose told Alva about helping Effie with her chores, and about the haint stories. Alva said she believed in haints, and she was pretty sure she believed in omens, too.

"Ghosts are scary," Rose said. "I don't think I'd ever want to meet one." She watched Alva's quick hands carve out the brown places on the apples. Alva threw the rotten parts in a basket for their pigs.

"I'd purely rather meet a ghost any day than a wolf," Alva said. "A wolf chased me of a night, just after the shivaree."

"Really?" Rose asked doubtfully. She had gotten used to people telling her tales. Mr. Stubbins did and so did Abe. Rose loved a tall tale, but she wanted to know when one was tall and when it was true.

"Ain't no lie about it," Alva said with a shiver. "I get chill bumps just a-studying on it. I was a-walking over to the Deavers', on t'other side of the railroad tracks. Mr. Deaver's cow got sick and died, and Missus Deaver got herself a new little baby boy.

"So my mama sent me over with a pail of milk after supper, when it was dark. I was a-walking through the woods and I heared a dog a-barking. But I knowed my papa weren't out a-hunting coons or fox, and it weren't no dog I ever heared afore. I could tell most any dog around just a-hearing its mouth.

"Then I heared it a-howling and I knowed it weren't no dog at all. I commenced a-walking fast as I could, a-being careful for the milk not to spill."

Rose could feel the hair bristle on the back of her neck. She took another sip of cider, to wet her lips.

"That old wolf was a-coming, Rose. I heared him bark real close. I stopped and listened. At first, all I could hear was my own heart a-drumming fast as a rabbit's. But then, plain as anything, I heared its feet a-running and a-rustling in the leaves."

"What did you do?" Rose asked breathlessly. Her heart was pounding, too.

Alva laughed. "I ran!" she shouted. "I ran with all my might, a-spilling milk all over. I was near a-giving up, when I seen a bit of yellow light from the Deavers' windows!

"I ran like a rabbit, but when I got near to the house, I stubbed my foot on a root and fell. A big gulp of milk spilled. I got up and ran to the door and banged on it.

"Afore Missus Deaver could come and open it, I looked back and there it was, that old wolf a-lapping up the milk, his bushy tail a-wagging like an old cur dog. Then Mr. Deaver's hunting dogs took up a-yapping and the wolf ran off."

Rose tingled all over. Alva was right. No ghost or haint could ever be as terrifying as being chased by a wolf.

"How did you get home?" Rose wanted to know.

Alva grabbed the last apple from the bottom of the basket, and hacked away at it.

"Mr. Deaver let his dogs loose on the wolf, and he rode me home on his horse. My papa and him went out three nights a-tracking it, but they never did see it. Papa 'lowed as it were just a lone wolf, a-looking for its pack, and got hungry when it scented the milk. Papa says wolves ain't got a name to hurt folks. Mostly they eat the stock, chickens and hogs and such."

Rose could not stop thinking about Alva's story as she helped Papa when it was their turn to make cider. Each time the catch-bucket filled with cider she helped Mama pour it into their barrel through a cloth that strained out bugs and bits of apple.

Rose tasted everyone's cider, and everyone took turns tasting one another's. Rose discovered that each kind of apple, from each orchard, had a different flavor. Some were smooth and sweet, and some were so strong and sour they made her mouth pucker.

But all of it was good, and fun to drink slowly, savoring the rich flavor. Cider wasn't something to gulp down like water. And a cider pressing was an entertainment, a time of friendship and kindness and laughter.

When they were done, they had pressed thirty gallons of cider. Papa gave five of those gallons to Mr. Stubbins for the use of his cider press. Another ten gallons was for the Bairds. Papa couldn't pay Abe cash money for all his work on Rocky Ridge Farm. Abe earned shares of the crops—corn and oats and timber-ing—and of the cider. That left fifteen gallons for Rose's family. They would drink as much as they could before it turned. Papa would let some of it ferment into hard cider, a grown-up drink. Mama would let the rest make itself into vinegar.

The cider pressing ended too soon. Rose wanted more time with Alva. She asked Mama if she could visit Alva on Sunday, after dinner.

"We ought to be finished with the corn by then," Mama said as they drove home. Rose sat in the wagon-box, leaning her back against the barrel of sloshing cider. "I don't see why not, so long as you're back in time for evening chores."

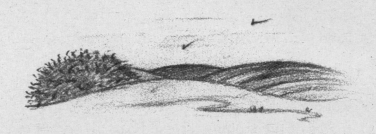

Beyond the Horizon

The next three days they cut and shocked corn. Rose woke in the pale light before dawn to find that a thick fog had sneaked up while she slept and swallowed the whole world. Rose heard Papa's footsteps and the door closing. She slid her bare feet out of bed onto the cold floor of her upstairs room and ran to the window.

Swinging from Papa's hand as he walked to the barn, the lantern made a fuzzy golden halo around him. As he walked away he disappeared into the fog until Rose could see only the bouncing, swinging light, and could hear his footsteps. And then the light too was devoured by the mist.

The fog was lovely, and strange. It turned everything familiar and friendly into a lurking mystery. Rose knew the barn was still there, and the old log house that Papa had made into a stall for Bunting and her calf. She could hear the mules braying for their breakfast, and the chickens fluttering and cackling awake in the henhouse.

But she couldn't see farther than the oak tree near the corner of the house, and it was just a shadow of itself. She kept remembering Alva's story about being followed home by a wolf, and Effie's haint tales. Rose wanted to use the convenience, but she waited until Papa came back from the barn so she could have the lantern.

After breakfast the sun burned off the fog. The day bloomed clear and bright, and they went to work in the corn. The air smelled clean and refreshing, spiced with the scent of dry grass and corn shuck, and it was full of tumbling red and yellow leaves that reminded Rose of butterflies scurrying to find a last bit of nectar.

Rose was grateful that the oveny days of summer had ended: no more chigger bites and hot sleepless nights. The cool, dry air, with just a hint of winter in it, woke her all up and sent her cheerfully to work under a warming sun in a velvety sky.

In the mornings just a few dazzling cloud castles sailed across it. In the afternoons after dinner the clouds scurried off, leaving a perfectly seamless bowl of pure blue light shining down on the earth.

At sundown, the breezes turned sharply cold with the first nip of frost. Rose put on her union suit under her dress before she went out to do evening chores. The moon, just a sliver from full, orangey-pink and streaked with shredded clouds, slowly lifted above the dark horizon over Patterson's Hill. Then it quickly soared into the clear night sky, spilling its milky light over the cornfield so they could go back to work. It was bright enough that Papa didn't even have to light the lanterns.

His ghostly shape and Abe's, made soft as

moss by the moon, moved through the field, cutting. Rose could hear the *whack*s of their hatchets, followed by the rattle of falling stalks. Rose, Mama, Effie, and Swiney followed down the rows, gathering up the top-heavy stalks. Mama carefully leaned them together in shocks that could stand up to the strongest breeze.

The crisp air carried every little night noise from the woods around. From a distant hollow came the wild baying of dogs hot on the trail of a fox or a raccoon. A gust of wind loosened acorns that fell and struck tree limbs with a loud *knock!* A horned owl cried out nearby, and farther away, another answered.

Swiney tried to imitate the owl's cry. "Whooo, who, who, who."

"Hush up!" Effie scolded him. "You want to get the Wilders' house burnt up?"

"Whatever do you mean?" Mama asked. She was holding some stalks, waiting for Rose and Swiney to bring her more to make a new shock.

"It's a sign," Effie said, huffing with an arm-load of corn. "Iffen you hear an owl a-crying, could be there's sickness a-coming down the road. And iffen you call out to an owl and it answers back, it might come down your chimney of a night and spread the coals out on the floor so your house burns up."

"You can't believe that, can you?" Mama said. "You're making a joke on me."

"No'm," Effie said earnestly. "I mean, I ain't seen it my own self, but that's what folks says. Owls is a bad token."

"I ain't afraid of no owls," Swiney said. And he called out again, "Whoooey, who, who, who."

Neither was Rose afraid. But she was glad she wasn't out in that field by herself. Rose knew every inch of it. She had helped plant and hoe it, and she often played in it with Swiney and Fido and Blackfoot. She knew the patches where the raccoons and oppossums had climbed up the stalks to steal the tender ears of corn. She knew where a groundhog had dug a hole, and where the quail left little hollows in the bare earth after taking their dust baths.

But at night, in the dreamy gray light, nothing was where or how she knew it. The field seemed to stretch out into the darkness as far as she could see, as endless as the sky. When she stood up to stretch her achy back, Rose stayed still a moment, listening and looking at the moon-washed earth. She could feel herself melting and disappearing, becoming part of the unknowable night.

Finally the corn was all shocked, and it was Sunday. As soon as the last dinner dish had been put away, Rose dashed upstairs to change into her everyday dress. Then she ran through the drifting leaves and along Fry Creek to the Stubbinses'. She didn't even stop to shake down the persimmons from the tree along the creek bank, to see if they were sweet yet.

Rose felt as wound up as a puppy let free after being cooped up a long time. She raced across the barnyard, scattering the flock of snowy geese, and burst into the Stubbinses' warm, steamy kitchen. There wasn't another house besides her own that she dared enter so boldly. But the Stubbinses were nearly family.

She knew the latchstring was always out for her.

Mrs. Stubbins stood over the cookstove, stirring a big pot of something. She looked up in surprise, her pleasant round face pink from the heat.

"Howdy!" Rose cried out.

"Why, look who's here!" Mrs. Stubbins declared in her big voice brimming with laughter. She brushed back strands of gray hair that clung to her shining cheek, put one hand on her hip and stirred with the other.

"You catched me, Rose," she said playfully. "A-working on Sunday! You ain't a-going to tittle-tattle to Reverend Ritchey, now, is you? He's all the time a-preaching agin work on the Lord's day."

"No," Rose said with a giggle. "I won't. What are you cooking? It smells good." In the corner on a stool sat Alva's little sister, Edith, feeding spoonfuls of scraped apple to her baby brother, Orville.

"I'm a-fixing a batch of grape jelly." Mrs. Stubbins chuckled, wiping her hands on her apron. "Them fox grapes don't know one day from t'other. You got to pick 'em afore they catch a frost and cook 'em quick, or they don't set up proper."

The door burst open and Alva flew in, gasping for breath. "I seen you, Rose. But I was a-chasing a rabbit, down in the cow pasture. Come on! I think I got it cornered. We can still catch it."

Alva grabbed Rose's hand and dragged her out of the house, Rose calling out a hurried, "Good-bye, Mrs. Stubbins!" as she stumbled after.

They looked under the big brush pile where Alva said the rabbit had run to hide. They climbed up on the springy mountain of sticks and branches and jumped up and down, laughing and trying to flush the rabbit out. But it never showed itself.

"Take me where you saw the wolf," Rose pleaded.

They walked over a hill and through a shallow valley to the far edge of the Stubbinses' farm. Mr. Stubbins owned one hundred forty acres of land, more than twice the size of Rocky Ridge

Farm. There were three whole fields of corn, all tidily shocked. In one of them a flock of crows, as busy as ants, strutted back and forth through the stubble hunting for fallen kernels.

Finally they came to the rail line, which was at the edge of the farm. They climbed the steep embankment of loose sooty stones and earth and stood for a moment, catching their breath, looking down the silver rails and listening.

Beyond the tracks stretched the Ozark hills, waves of unbroken forest as far as Rose could see. They were up high there, on the highest place in the mountains.

Rose knew the lonely cries of the train whistles and the *clickity-clack* of the wheels as surely as she knew the clatter of a pot lid when she woke in the morning. She heard them day and night, like the background sounds of roosters crowing in the barnyard or the rhythm of Papa's axe chopping in the woodlot. And whenever the train whistle sounded, there were always the howls of neighboring dogs to answer it. Those sounds were a comfort, telling a story of life going on.

But this was the first time Rose had ever been this close. The air there smelled tarry and smoky. The cross-ties were slippery with oil and gritty with coal dust. Those cross-ties were the same as the cross-ties that Papa and Abe spent winters hacking out of their trees to sell to the railroad. Papa might have made the very cross-tie she was standing on.

Rose trembled with excitement as they stepped across the gleaming rails to the other side of the embankment. It was something to imagine; a big locomotive could come thundering across that very place at any moment.

Alva showed Rose where she first had heard the wolf, and told again how she could hear its feet rustling in the leaves, and how it almost caught up to her before she got to the Deavers' house. When she got to the part where she tripped and fell, Alva suddenly pointed into the woods and shouted, "Sakes alive, Rose! It's here!"

Rose screamed, and her heart leaped into her mouth. She looked where Alva was pointing but didn't see a wolf. Then Alva was laughing and laughing, holding her stomach. Rose's fright quickly turned to embarrassment and then, in the next instant, to white fury. She blushed hard and without a thought shoved Alva down. Alva landed with a thud that knocked her breath out.

Alva's face puckered to cry, and she glared hard at Rose. But then she began to laugh again, rolling in the leaves.

"I'm sorry, Rose," she said, her face blazing crimson. "I was just a-funning you. You oughta seed your face. I got your goat that time."

Rose turned and stalked off, back toward the tracks. She could hear Alva walking behind her, but she refused to turn around. She hugged her anger to herself until the heat of her boiling heart slowly cooled. When she scrambled back up the grade to the rail line, she stopped and listened and looked down the tracks. Far off to the east she heard the faint cry of a whistle.

"A train's coming!" she cried out. Alva huffed up the stony slope. They both listened for a moment.

"Look, Rose. You can hear it in the tracks." Alva knelt down by one of the rails and pressed her ear against it. Rose hunkered down and did the same. Tiny rumbling noises echoed in her ear, as if she were hearing them through a long tunnel. Those were the sounds of the wheels on the track!

The whistle cried again, a little bit louder, but still far off. Rose wanted to see the train up close, so she sat on a rail and waited for it to come. Alva walked along the tracks with her head bowed as if she was searching for something.

Rose got impatient. She picked a bouquet of asters from a patch that tumbled like a purple waterfall down the embankment. She watched the black-and-orange monarch butterflies hurrying by without stopping, and found a woolly bear caterpillar humping along one of the rails. Rose picked it off and set it on the ground so the train couldn't squash it.

A flock of flickers, their white rump patches flashing, hunted ants in a patch of grass. A hawk's shadow flitted across the ground, and they all flew up into a tree, scolding in their strident voices.

Rose looked down the tracks. Alva had her ear down on a rail again. Then she jumped up and came running back to Rose, her braids flying.

"It's a-coming," she said breathlessly. "Look, I found these." She held out an open hand. There were two rusty nails in it. "We can put 'em on the track, and when the train comes, it'll mash 'em flat." She laid them one across the other, in an X.

Then Rose spied a smudge of black smoke in the clear blue sky at the horizon. She could hear the *chuff*ing now, sharp and loud, and the rumble of the cars. Something fluttered in her chest.

"We'd best get off the tracks," Rose said. "It's close now." She ran down the embankment. But Alva stayed where she was between the tracks, staring down the rails.

"Alva, come on!" Rose pleaded. "The train's coming. You could get hurt."

Alva scoffed. "I done this a hunnert times. You can see it a long time afore it's a-coming. I seen boys stand here 'til the train near run 'em down. They jump off at the last second."

Rose sighed and scrambled back up the embankment. There was nowhere to run to up there, unless you flew back down the embankment. But then she spied a flat place near the rail bed, a little bit down the tracks. She ran to that spot and stood waiting.

The coming train cried out again, very loud now. Down the tracks there was a curve. Rose stared at it, waiting for the locomotive to come tearing around the corner. Alva followed, walking on one of the rails, her arms held out for balance. Little wisps of her red hair fluttered in the breeze.

"It's an express. Number Six, the Stockman's Special, a-going to Kansas City all the way from Memphis," Alva said, concentrating on her bare feet as she wobbled her way down the narrow rail.

"How can you know that?"

"I been a-living by this here railroad since I was birthed," she said, hopping off in front of Rose. "I know ever' train by ear and I can tell this one's a-going too lickety-split to be a-stopping in town. Expresses don't stop in Mansfield. It's too small. And Number Six comes by ever' day afore evening chores."

The tracks suddenly gave out a pinging noise that startled Rose. She looked down the rails and saw the great engine swing into view, its bright headlight glaring at them through the quivering air. A river of black smoke gushed from its stack.

"It's coming awfully fast," Rose said.

Alva moved away from the rails to stand by Rose. Rose grabbed Alva's hand. She felt her heart racing faster and faster. She looked at those rails, at the rusty nails perched on top, so close in front of her, just a few feet away, about to be crushed by the fierce iron monster.

The locomotive grew bigger and bigger. It seemed to pick up speed as it got closer. She felt it bearing down on them, its black face sneering with contempt, its wide black stack like a top hat belching its angry breath. Her legs ached to run.

A plume of white steam poured out of the top

of the engine, and an instant later the air quivered with the shriek of its whistle. An echo answered from the surrounding hills. A whirling cloud of dust and leaves billowed out along the sides of the track, and now Rose could see the wooden cars that followed the engine, rocking from side to side, snaking along behind.

A wave of delicious terror tingled her spine and crinkled over her scalp. The deafening thunder and rumble and clatter was the loudest noise she'd ever heard. She could even feel it quaking the earth.

The rails cried out, screeching. Rose opened her mouth to scream with delight, but she could barely hear herself above the racket.

Then the train hurtled past. For an instant she saw a man in a striped hat and overalls waving to them from the engine's cab. Then a gust of wind slapped Rose's face. It grabbed and tore at her skirt and braids as though it wanted to drag her under the wicked sharp wheels. She squeezed Alva's hand.

The cars rumbled and rattled past in a blur—one, two, three boxcars and then two

passenger cars, with people sitting at the windows. The gleaming rails rose and fell slightly as the wheels passed singing over them. Rose caught fleeting pictures: a woman in a large feathered hat; a man reading a newspaper with a cigar in his mouth; a little boy in a sailor suit tossing a piece of paper out the window.

Then the last car passed, and Rose was blinded by a cyclone of filthy air, gray and thick. A fine rain of greasy soot and clinker dust fell all over her and stung her eyes. She covered her face with her hands. She could taste the bitter coal smoke on her lips.

Finally the wind of the train died, and Rose could see again. The train clattered away down the tracks, the last car wobbling a little, growing smaller and smaller. Two little girls in white dresses stood in the rear door, waving to them. The cloud of smoke and dust thinned and drifted away across the fields. The engine let out another fierce shriek; then it disappeared around the curve into town.

"Ow!" Alva complained. "Let go my hand, Rose. You're a-hurting it."

Rose laughed uncontrollably. Nothing in all her life—not the shivaree or exploring Williams Cave or crossing the Missouri River—had ever been so thrilling and terrifying. Nothing had ever made her feel so tingly and alive.

That night as she lay in her bed waiting for sleep, Rose ran a finger over the smooth flat cross that the train wheels had made of those rusty nails. They were smashed so flat that they had become one piece of metal.

From far away came the faint wail of a train whistle. Rose loved that lonely cry. It made her feel a pleasant sort of sadness without having anything at all to be sad about, and a kind of wanting, without knowing that she wanted something.

Rose thought about the trains and wondered about the great cities they were always hurrying off to: Memphis, St. Louis, Kansas City, Chicago, even New York. Where was that little boy going, and where had he come from?

She thought about how, at that very moment, people were sitting on a train, rushing past

Rocky Ridge Farm, on important and mysterious journeys to far-off places that Rose had never seen. She had traveled far and wide in her books and in the newspapers she read. She had traveled all the way from South Dakota in a covered wagon with Mama and Papa. But now, for the first time, she began to wonder what lay around the bend in the tracks, beyond the horizon.

Rose remembered something she had read in *Robinson Crusoe*, that Crusoe "had a mind to see the world." She decided that that book was more than just a story. It was a lesson that spoke to her. She had a mind to see the world, too. Some day, when she was grown up, she was going to do just that.

Butchering Time

The first frosts came to the mountains and lay white on the fields each morning. The ground froze hard underfoot. Each night carved another little slice from the full moon. Then, when the moon was in the last quarter, when every day dawned icy cold and all the flies were dead, it was butchering time.

Mama and Papa didn't have hogs to butcher. Since they had come to the Ozarks they had bought their meat, or Papa traded fence rails for it.

"Seems hardly worth the bother to raise

your own hog and have to worry about it getting stolen or sick or lost in the woods," Papa had said. "And look at the trouble they make. Every time you turn around they're getting their noses into somebody's business."

This year Mr. Stubbins was going to give them some of his meat, because his hogs had broken into Papa's cornfield in the summer and had eaten up a whole corner of it.

The Ozarks was free-range country. Farmers didn't fence their hogs in. They let them run free in the woods until fall, when they gentled and fattened them with corn. Wild hogs were a terrible bother. A family of wild hogs had stripped the bark off some of the little orchard trees in their first fall on the farm.

Now Mr. Stubbins owed Papa the meat in return for the lost corn. But Mama, Papa, and Rose would help with the butchering. It was a neighborly thing to do.

Rose had never been to a hog-killing, but she didn't like the sound of it or the look on Mama's face when Papa told them about it.

"He's got a mess of butchering to do," Papa

said at breakfast. "I reckon there'll be eight big hogs to dress and render."

Mama sighed heavily as she served herself another spoonful of sliced turnips. "I believe I'd sooner clean out stalls every day for a year then spend a single morning grinding sausage and rendering fat."

It was a bitter-cold windy day. A thick blanket of dirty gray clouds scudded across the sky just above the treetops. Rose huddled down in the wagon-box in her heavy coat, her fascinator tied tight around her head. But still she could not make herself warm.

Mama had brought a pile of clean flour sacks to wrap the meat in, all her extra crocks, a washpan, and even the butter churn for sausage meat.

Rose helped Papa unhitch the team in the barnyard, and then he went straight off to the other side of the barn where Mr. Stubbins, Abe, Swiney, and some men from neighboring farms were getting ready to slaughter. Rose hurried to the house with Mama, anxious to get into the Stubbinses' warm, cozy kitchen.

Alva showed Rose and Mama where to put their coats, in the bedroom across the dogtrot. They threw them on top of the big pile of coats and fascinators on the bed. Then they dashed across the windy dogtrot into the big welcoming kitchen.

Mrs. Stubbins, Effie, Mrs. Deaver, who had brought her little boy, and two other women Rose had not met before bustled about in their oldest work dresses and aprons, preparing food, feeding fires, and chattering like a flock of jaybirds.

Alva's little sister, Edith, was chasing two other little girls around the big heavy table, until Mrs. Stubbins scolded them and sent them upstairs to play. The air was smoky and thick. The cookstove, already roaring hot, was covered with steaming pots of water. A black kettle hung in the fireplace over a blazing fire.

Mama, Alva, and Rose sat at the big kitchen table, cutting onions and wiping away the stinging tears with the hems of their aprons. When a mountain of crisp white onions had been cut and sliced up, they peeled potatoes.

"You want to go out and watch 'em kill the hogs?" Alva asked. "It's something to see."

"No," Rose said quickly. "I don't even like to see Mama kill a chicken." Rose loved pork meat and she loved chicken, and she knew butchering was something that had to be done. But she did not like to see any creature killed, not even a woolly bear caterpillar.

They sliced and cut and peeled all morning. When most of it was done, Alva ran outside to watch the butchering. Rose stayed inside and played with Mrs. Deaver's baby. He was lying in bedclothes in an old crate in the corner, his bright blue eyes watching a bit of yellow yarn that Rose dangled over his face.

"What's his name?" Rose asked.

"Vearl," Mrs. Deaver said proudly. "That was his grandpa's name. He was a colonel in the War Between the States."

Vearl's wet little mouth puckered. Then he gurgled and smiled at Rose with eyes as deep as a clear autumn sky. His plump little cheeks looked so soft and velvety that Rose just had to bend down and kiss him. The skin felt

88

smoother and softer than flower petals, and he smelled wonderfully fresh. His little bonnet was crooked, so Rose straightened it for him.

"Why don't you hold him a spell?" Mrs. Deaver said. "He's taken to you right quick."

Rose carefully picked the baby up, cradling his bottom and being extra careful to hold his head up the way she had seen other people do it. Vearl's tiny fists waved helplessly and he kicked with his feet.

Rose jiggled him a little and hummed a verse of "Buffalo Gals." He stopped squirming, and his eyes grew big and looked deep into Rose's, as if searching for something there. She just loved that little baby.

But then his face squeezed into a frown, and he began to fuss.

"What's wrong?" Rose asked worriedly.

"I reckon he's a-wanting to suck," Mrs. Deaver said with a sigh. "He's all the time hungry. I never did see a creature eat as much." She gently took Vearl from Rose's arms, hefted him onto her shoulder, and went through the door to the bedroom.

Rose wanted to follow Mrs. Deaver and watch her nurse Vearl, but she was too shy to ask. She had not been around babies very much, and there were many things she did not understand about them.

Just then Abe came in carrying a washpan piled up with purple-red meat.

"Here's the livers," he called out cheerfully. He gave the pan to Mrs. Stubbins and hurried back out the door. Mrs. Stubbins and Effie quickly sliced the livers into strips. They laid the pieces, with some drippings, in a big hot fry pan, and the meat began to sizzle. The kitchen filled with a delicious smell.

When the liver was browned, Mrs. Stubbins filled the pan with the sliced onions and put on the lid so it would simmer.

Then Mr. Stubbins brought in two long backbones with lots of meat still on. Those went into the big black kettle of boiling water in the fireplace. After they had boiled for a time, Rose and Alva helped cut up heads of cabbage to slip into the pot with the backbones.

Then they mixed biscuit dough, and took

turns stirring the beans to keep them from burning and sticking to the bottom of the pot. Mrs. Stubbins kept checking the kettle of backbones and nervously looking out the window toward the barn.

"All right, girls," she finally called out. "It lacks just a little bit of the menfolk a coming in. Thank goodness the backbones are done!"

There was a great rush now to set the table and put out the open jars of blackberry jam and plum butter and pickled watermelon and corn relish. Rose went around the heavy, long table and carefully centered a plate at each place, and straightened the silverware, and set a cup to the left of each plate.

Then came the steaming fragrant platters of boiled backbones and cabbage, fried liver and onions, a big bowl of coleslaw, and more bowls of stewed tomatoes, bubbling brown beans with molasses, fried hominy, potatoes beaten with butter, and mashed sweet potatoes with brown sugar melted on top. Rose sneaked a swipeful of the golden sweet potatoes on her finger. They melted in her mouth.

There were plates piled up with squares of cornbread and round biscuits, a big dish of sleek butter, pitchers of smooth milk gravy, and buttermilk to drink.

There were so many bowls and platters that some of them had to be perched on top of others to make room. The whole table steamed, and the windows ran with sweat.

Rose didn't understand what was so terrible about butchering day. So far it seemed like a wonderful feast.

Then the men came clumping in, bringing a gust of refreshing cold air. Rose was damp from all that heat, and the faces of the women were pink from bending over stoves and stoking fires.

The men's noses blazed red from the cold. They rubbed their raw hands together to warm them, laughing and jostling each other as they took turns washing in the pan on a chair by the door, and then drying their hands on the roller towel.

Mr. Stubbins went to the head of the groaning table and stood looking over all those dishes.

"Well, boys," he said grandly. "I see the ladies whipped me up a little snack. You fellas can watch me eat, or I reckon we might scrounge you up a a few crumbs of stale corn-pone and some drippings."

"You quit a-beating your gums, Emmett, and let these men eat their dinner," Mrs. Stubbins cried out over the hearty laughter of the men. "Or a hunk o' tailbone is all you'll get."

The kitchen exploded with laughter again, chairs scraped, and the men all sat down to eat.

Swiney raced around the table, looking for a chair.

"Just where do you think you're a-going?" Effie said, an eyebrow arching as she set a bubbling hot apple pie on the table.

"I'm eating with the men!" Swiney declared. "I helped slaughter, didn't I?"

"You ain't big enough yet," said Effie. "You can just wait like the rest of the young-uns and womenfolk."

"Awww, heck!" Swiney scowled, his cheeks still flushed with cold. "I'll never be big enough."

"Shucks, Effie. Let the little feist sit." Mr. Stubbins chuckled. "Ain't no other boys to wait, and he can sit on the salt barrel."

Swiney pushed the tall salt barrel in between Abe and Mr. Stubbins and climbed up on it. He sat up high, higher than anyone else, beaming with pride to be eating with the grown-up men. His eyes swept the table with the greedy look a hungry crow gives a cornfield it's about to rob.

The kitchen filled now with the cozy sounds of clattering plates and silverware, and the joking and satisfied humming of hungry people filling the emptiness inside them.

Rose wanted to sit with the grown-up men too. It was hard to just stand and watch them spear the juicy bits of meat, spoon up the bright vegetables, pour the rich gravy, and devour all that delicious food. Mama and the other women hurried around the room, skirts billowing, dabbing the dampness from their foreheads with their aprons, refilling bowls and pitchers, and pouring coffee.

Everyone was hungry, of course. But there

never could be enough platters and plates for everyone to eat at once, and the table was only so big. The men always ate first at a butchering or a threshing or a log-rolling. The women always waited, although Rose wondered why it was so. The women worked just as hard.

When the men had polished off two apple pies and drunk their coffee and lit their pipes, they went back to work, and the women could finally sit. The liver was delicious and rich, smothering in sweet, browned onions and gravy. Mrs. Stubbins had held back a dried-peach pie. She gave Rose a big slice, with a pool of silky cream dripping all down the sides. Rose ate and ate until every corner of her was stuffed.

After the dinner dishes had been washed, the women began the hard kitchen work. The men had been outside in the yard, butchering the meat into hams, shoulders, middlings, and jowls that they covered all over with salt and packed into crates and barrels and sacks.

All the pieces of fat came into the kitchen. The pieces with a little bit of lean in them had to be ground up in the sausage mill that was clamped to the kitchen table. The women took turns cranking the handle while Rose and Alva stuffed in the meat. Then Mrs. Stubbins and Effie seasoned the meat with pepper and salt and sage, and began to cook it into patties.

The pieces that were all fat they cut up into cubes. Everyone sat around the table cutting and cutting mountains of fat into cubes. It was a greasy, messy job, and Rose could see why Mama didn't like it. It seemed there was no place on her that wasn't greasy, or in the kitchen, either. The table and even the floor grew slippery with it. Rose wondered if she would ever get clean again.

When all the fat had been cubed, they dumped it into another big black kettle that stood outside in the yard over a slow fire. It was Rose and Alva's job to keep stirring the melting fat with a long wooden paddle, stirring and stirring to keep it from burning, until it was cooked just right.

Gusts of wind blew smoke and ash in their faces, and their feet got clammy and cold.

They took turns, one stirring while the other warmed herself by the fire. They hardly spoke, they were so miserable out there. Mrs. Stubbins came out of the house every little while to peek at the cooking lard and fix the fire.

When she finally came out and said the lard was cooked just right, she doused the fire. She brought old flour sacks out of the house, and Mama and the other women lugged over the big stone crocks that everyone had brought. Mrs. Stubbins dipped the cooling lard into the sacks with a ladle. Then they all stood around squeezing and squeezing those sacks to squeeze the greasy white lard out into the crocks. That was even messier than cutting the fat had been.

Finally, when all the lard had been squeezed out, only the cracklings were left. Crackling was deliciously crisp and salty like bacon, and Mama would fry some of it up to mix in with her cornbread. But most of it she would cook with lye water to make their soap.

It was nearly dark when they finished, and

the air was biting cold. Papa had gone back to the farm with Swiney to feed and water the livestock. Then he came to fetch Rose and Mama. Rose was tired and shivery and covered with grease. She was sick of the smell of pork fat, and sick of butchering.

They loaded the wagon with the churn full of lard, and sacks and sacks of salted hams and shoulders and white meat, and the backbones, and some pork chops that were eat-now meat, and sausage meat, spareribs, crackling to be made into lye soap, and more slabs of fat that Mama said they would have to cook down to make the rest of their lard, and the head to be made into souse, and even the feet to be pickled.

"The only part of the hog that gets wasted is the squeal," Mama joked in a tired voice. "Tomorrow we'll put up the sausage and then start rendering the rest of the fat."

Rose was too cold and tired and cranky even to moan a complaint. She just huddled against the cold and grumbled to herself as the wagon bumped along the track through the dark woods toward home.

The Tam o' Shanter

For two whole days they cooked and canned. Mama fried up all the sausage into patties. Then she put the patties into stone jars and poured warm lard over them. She set the jars upside down in a pan on the porch, so the lard would drip down and seal the jar's open mouth.

When the lard had cooled and turned solid as wax, she turned each jar over, stretched a bit of cloth over the top, and tied it tight with a string. Then the sausage was sealed and would keep a long time in the smokehouse. They would have sausage all winter and even into the spring.

They cooked up another batch of lard, and Mama canned the backbones and ribs. All the canned meat and the salted meat, everything except the eat-now pork chops that they had for dinner and supper, went into the smoke-house. Then, when the souse was made and the feet pickled, the work was done and they scrubbed the kitchen floor with sand and lye soap to get out all the spilled grease.

Butchering was hateful work, but now they had meat to last almost the whole year. The harvest was finished.

Thanksgiving came, and the Cooleys spent the cold blustery day on Rocky Ridge Farm. Mr. and Mrs. Cooley were Mama and Papa's best friends, and Paul and George, their sons, had been Rose's friends since she was a little girl in South Dakota. Paul was twelve and a half years old and George was ten.

Mr. Cooley ran the Mansfield Hotel in town, on the square. Mrs. Cooley did the cooking and washing, and Paul and George helped with the chores. But Mr. Cooley told Papa and Mama he was going to quit the hotel.

"It's no place to raise a family," he complained, pouring gravy over a slice of the turkey Papa had shot. "The sort of people you have around a hotel, traveling men and the like. Not what I like to subject a family to, if you know what I mean."

"Of course," said Mama. "I never did like living in towns. So much noise, and hardly any privacy."

"What'll you do, then?" asked Papa.

"I've got it all worked out," Mr. Cooley said. "The railroad is taking me on as a freight agent at the depot, and I still have my wagon and team. So I can keep myself busy the rest of the time with drayage, hauling shipments from the trains."

"And we're going to have a real house!" plump Mrs. Cooley declared, her dancing eyes bright with happiness. "Maybe even with a parlor. Oh, how I have pined for a parlor."

After dinner the children went upstairs to Rose's new room to play.

"Let's have an election rally," Paul said. "You and George can be the voters, except you can't vote, Rose, 'cause you're a girl. I'll be the candidate."

"What's a rally? And who says a girl can't vote?" Rose demanded.

"A rally is for an election," said Paul. "Don't you know anything? To choose the president. And everybody knows girls can't vote."

Rose knew about the election, of course. She had read of it in the *Chicago Inter-Ocean*, a newspaper that Papa brought home from town sometimes. But those stories about the election bored her.

"The election is over, anyway," Rose said. "I know that." Mr. McKinley, the goldbug, had won, and now he was to be the new president. Mr. Bryan, who wanted free silver, had lost.

"Sure it is," Paul said. "But we can pretend. I'll make a speech, and you have to clap or laugh or boo. But you better not boo, 'cause I'm for free silver."

None of them knew what a goldbug was, or if free silver really meant that Mr. Bryan would have given everyone money. But Mama and Papa, and Mr. and Mrs. Cooley, were for free silver, so Paul made up a speech against the goldbugs.

He stood up and spoke, one hand tucked inside his shirt, while Rose and George sat on the rag rug and cheered, just the way Paul said they did in town at a rally before the election. Paul said the country was going to wrack and ruin, and the big men in Washington, and the businessmen in the cities, were the only folks to make money on it.

"Yaay!" yelled Rose and George.

"These goldbugs are nothing mor'n rich folks and merchants who want to keep down the common man and take the food from the mouths of the little babies," Paul bellowed, his voice as deep as he he could make it. "See the price of flour now, near nine dollars the barrel. If the goldbugs get in, the price'll go to twelve and the merchants'll suck the life out of your purse. It's free silver for the farmer and the little man!"

"Yaay!" Rose and George cheered and clapped, not knowing at all what they were cheering and clapping for.

After Thanksgiving, school took up again. The first morning, after the breakfast chores were done, Rose wriggled into her new dress, a Turkey-red calico sprigged with tiny yellow leaves and flowers that Mama had sewn up for her.

Rose had picked out the cloth at Reynolds' store with Mama. Alva had a dress made of the same calico, and Rose thought it looked so pretty on her that she wanted one just like it.

Mama had saved the tatted collar and cuffs from Rose's old dress and Rose had repaired the torn stitches herself. Papa even brought her home a new pair of Brogans. Mama gave her old patched pair to Swiney.

Rose had loved school in South Dakota, but school in Missouri was different. Sometimes Mama kept her home to help with the chores, but mostly the schoolwork bored Rose. She read so much by herself, and had studied so far in her lessons with Mama, that she was far ahead of the other scholars. Mama did not mind letting her stay home, so long as she kept up her lessons.

But after the constant hard work of harvest time, Rose was glad for a change, glad to dress up again and glad for the chance to see her good friend Blanche. She was excited too because she would finally move up to the Fourth Reader. Blanche was moving up also, and George Cooley would be in that same class.

Miss Pimberton taught the Fourth Reader. She was young and pretty, and she spoke in a soft gentle voice. Some of the older scholars had told Rose about Miss Pimberton, that she was very kind and pleasant.

Professor Kay, Rose's Third Reader teacher, had favored her, and Rose thought he told wonderful, funny stories. But she liked to have a woman teacher better.

Rose saddled her little donkey, Spookendyke, in the barn hallway and walked him to the porch of the house where she tethered him to the railing. Fido followed prancing, his tail wagging furiously, thinking Rose would take him with her for a romp in the woods.

Rose came inside to get her dinner bucket, tie on her fascinator, pull on her blue mittens, and kiss Mama good-bye. Mama walked with her out onto the porch. A fine mist had begun to fall, and Mama hugged herself against the raw, wintry air.

"It's bitter cold," she said pulling up the worn collar on Rose's heavy coat. "Are you warm enough?"

"Yes, Mama," Rose said, untethering Spookendyke. Then she hefted herself up into the saddle.

Mama looked out at the weather. "Mmmm," she said thoughtfully. "I wonder. . . . Well, what's the difference? Don't go just yet." Then she dashed inside.

Rose waited, full of curiosity.

In a flash, Mama was back, holding something in her hand, something made of blue cloth.

Her breath came in puffs of steam. "I was saving this for a surprise, but it's so cold and damp." She handed it to Rose.

Rose turned it over and over. It was a hat, floppy and made all of soft wool, lined with black cambric. On top a soft, fuzzy ball of black yarn had been sewn. The stitches in the hat were tiny, close together and perfectly spaced: Mama's sewing. Rose would recognize it anywhere.

"It's beautiful," Rose breathed. She quickly untied her fascinator and pulled the hat on her head. It fit a little loosely, but Mama said she could pull it down over her ears if it was extra cold out.

"How does it look?"

"Very cunning," Mama said with a big smile. She reached up and adjusted the floppy part. "I saw a picture of a girl wearing one in *The Ladies' World* magazine that Mrs. Cooley sent over. I had to guess just how it was made, without a pattern. But it looks just like the picture. It's called a tam o' shanter." The sound of it made Rose giggle.

"It's a hat a Scotsman might wear. You remember, our family came from Scotland to settle this country. The hat is named for a character in a poem written by a Scotsman, Robert Burns."

"Tammy Shanter is a person?"

"Tam o' Shanter." Mama corrected her. "It is a ghost story. In the poem it says that Tam o' Shanter galloped on his gray mare through the mud, 'Despising wind, and rain,' and 'holding fast his good blue bonnet.'

"So now you are a true Scotswoman, Rose, with a good blue bonnet."

Rose grinned with pleasure. Her dinner pail was packed with good things to eat, a sandwich of light bread and sausage with butter on the bread. She had on her new dress, new shoes, *and* a fine new hat. She would have nothing to be ashamed of before the town girls in school.

"Oh, Mama. Thank you soooo much," she crooned, leaning over in the saddle and giving Mama a noisy kiss on her chilled cheek.

"Go on and hurry now, or you'll be late."

Professor Crowe

The weather was so miserable that even Spookendyke was eager to reach the shelter of the hitching shed at school. He clomped quickly on his little stiff legs across the new wooden bridge Papa had built over Fry Creek. Then he hobbled up the path over Patterson's Hill. Under that hill was Williams Cave, which Rose had explored with Alva and with Paul and George. Then Spookendyke climbed down to the schoolhouse, which stood at the end of the street, overlooking the town.

Rose hitched Spookendyke in the wooden

shed with the other scholars' horses and mules and hurried inside the two-story brick school-house. Children poured in from every direction, the boys pushing and shoving, everyone laughing and shouting first-day greetings, tearing off their mittens and heavy coats, banging their dinner pails as they crowded into the classrooms.

Rose knew right where to go. She dashed up the staircase, clutching her slate and her pail, breathing in all the wonderful smells of newly waxed floors and fresh paint. She wanted to be sure to find a seat with Blanche.

Rose burst into the Fourth Reader room. In all the confusion of children taking off their coats and putting away their dinner pails, she could not see Blanche or Miss Pimberton or George Cooley or the Hibbard twins. She felt a moment of panic.

Then she spotted Blanche, sitting in the front row, next to another girl! Rose's heart sank. But then Blanche turned and spotted her. Her face lit up with a big grin. She jumped up and ran between the desks.

"Oh, Rose! I was worried you mightn't come," she gushed. Her shiny black hair was cleverly curled, and she was wearing a dress made of the most beautiful dark-blue velvet with white satin collar and cuffs, and a white satin sash.

"Hang your coat quick and put up your dinner pail. You must meet my cousin, Lydia. She's come from Chicago and she's staying with us this winter because she was sick and it's too much colder in Chicago. I saved a seat at the desk behind ours."

Rose was relieved as she carefully hung her new hat and coat in the girls' cloakroom and put her pail on the shelf. She did not fit in with the town girls, except for Blanche. Rose had worried that Blanche might stop being her friend and choose a new friend. But Lydia was Blanche's cousin. Of course Blanche should sit with her own kin.

At the last minute Rose decided to take off her pinafore, even though Mama would be cross if she knew. Rose hated to cover up her new dress, and the town girls almost never wore them. She folded it neatly and tucked it into the arm of her coat.

Rose slid into the desk behind Blanche, next to a girl wearing a brown-and-green gingham dress that was too short for her legs and let her tattered union suit show at the ankles. Her shoes were muddy, and one of the soles was loose, so Rose knew she was a country girl.

Her skin was dark brown, as if she had been in the sun, and she wore her dark brown hair in braids up high on the sides of her head, the way Rose had seen Indian girls wear it in pictures.

Rose reached down and tugged up the legs of her own union suit, so it wouldn't show.

"Hello," Rose said, raising her voice to be heard over the noise of the other scholars. She spied George Cooley wrestling with another boy over the dipper by the water bucket. "My name is Rose Wilder."

"I'm Lula Faddis," the girl said in a voice as syrupy as molasses. "I'm new 'round here. Y'all ever heared o' Lou-sianna? That's where my kin live. We growed cotton 'n' tobacky, but my pa cain't make no money in cotton, so we all come to Missourah. That sure is a right purty dress you got."

"Silence in the Fourth Reader!" A man's deep voice bellowed from the back of the room. Rose jumped at the suddenness of it, and instantly the room fell quiet, with a few last rattlings and scrapings of slates and shoes and desks.

Everyone spun around to see who had shouted. A tall man with a bushy black mustache, a bald head, and a long piece of cane in his hand scowled at them with fierce dark eyes. Harry Carnall sniggered in the stunned silence. The tall man's eyes fixed on him like a hawk's. He strode between the rows of desks, straight to Harry.

Every eye in the room grew wide and scared-looking, and the boys around Harry shrank away from him.

Without a word the tall man grabbed Harry by the neck and lifted him off his seat.

"Ow! Ow! Ow!" Harry cried out as the man dragged him in front of the class. Harry's face turned bright red and tears began to run down his face.

"I am Professor Crowe," the man said in a thundering voice. Harry squirmed and sniffled, his face puckered with pain. But Professor Crowe would not let go. He laid the cane on his desk, picked up a piece of chalk, and wrote his name on the chalkboard. Harry wriggled in his other hand like a grasshopper stuck on a fishhook.

"This is the Fourth Reader, and I am your teacher. Lest any one of you think me amusing, or find it entertaining to misbehave, you will discover what this young pup has learned. I will tolerate no foolishness!" he bellowed.

Rose scrunched down in her seat and rubbed the back of her neck. She could almost feel Professor Crowe's cruel hand. Where was kindly Miss Pimberton? Her spirits began to sink.

Finally Professor Crowe let poor Harry go. Harry stumbled to his seat, rubbing the back of his neck and loudly snuffling.

Professor Crowe picked up the bell on his desk and rang it so hard that the sound buzzed in

Rose's eardrums. "Take up your books!" he declared. There was shuffling everywhere as the scholars opened their readers. Blanche turned and looked at Rose with big, frightened eyes.

Lula didn't have a reader of her own, so she shared Rose's.

The old feeling Rose had of hating school came back to her with a sickening rush. She felt even worse than before, because Professor Crowe was mean. She didn't dare even write a note to Blanche on her slate.

She sat listening to the other students recite lessons she already knew by heart. Professor Crowe struck his desk hard with the cane switch when someone spoke out of turn or made a mistake. It made a terribly loud *crack!* that frightened Rose and made her skin crawl and burn hot.

She stared at the back of Lydia's head. Her hair was as yellow as buttercups, and long and loose, with a beautiful soft curl at the bottom where it touched her shoulders. Her green serge dress was trimmed with velvet, and on her wrist she wore a gold-colored bracelet.

Rose wondered if she would ever dress as finely as the town girls.

Finally it was time for recess and all the students grabbed their coats to go outside, even though the weather was cold and and a light rain was still falling. No one wanted to stay inside with Teacher. Rose stood shivering by a corner of the schoolhouse with Blanche and Lydia. Some of the boys were playing Anty Over at the hitching shed, making cawing sounds like crows.

"Oh, he's just awful!" Blanche wailed.

"What happened to Miss Pimberton?" Rose wondered.

"She got married and moved away. I don't know how I'll ever bear it to get through the whole Fourth Reader."

"I wish I was back in Chicago," Lydia said mournfully. Her wool coat had a beautiful collar of dark brown fur that she turned up to cover her neck. "Father would never let me go to a school with such a spiteful teacher."

After recess they worked on their ciphering, writing answers to problems on their slates.

Professor Crowe stalked up and down the rows of desks, slapping his cane switch against his leg. In the middle of a problem, "Three times twelve," he stopped at Rose's desk. Rose was too frightened to look up.

"Where in the world did you learn to write like that?" he said.

Rose looked at her hand and arm, which were turned sideways to the slate. Ever since she was little in school in South Dakota she had written that way because she sat on the left of a girl who was left-handed. There had been no room to write the way the other scholars did. So she had learned to turn in her seat and write sideways.

"Well?" Professor Crowe's deep voice boomed out. "I am waiting for your answer."

Rose sat still as a statue, not knowing what to say, feeling every eye in the room staring at her.

Finally she managed to answer in a croaking whisper, "It's only the way I learned, in my old school."

"You are not in your old school any longer,"

Professor Crowe quickly said. "You will write with your elbow at your side, sitting in the proper manner in your seat, or I shall have to tie your arm down until you learn."

Then he walked slowly on down the row of desks, the switch slapping his leg. Rose stared at her slate, at the rows of numbers, and a wild feeling blew up inside her. She hated to be made fun of in front of the class. And she hated to be told what to do. Her spelling was perfect, and so was her penmanship. It didn't matter how she wrote. She could write hanging upside down in a tree if she wanted to.

The rest of that day was as awful as the morning, except that Rose stayed in at dinnertime and read from one of the books in the little library in the corner of the room: *Gulliver's Travels*. She read about Gulliver getting tied up by the Lilliputians. Rose thought that was what she'd like to do with Professor Crowe. But soon she was carried away by the story and she forgot her cares. Whenever Rose was troubled, a good story would make her feel better.

In the afternoon Professor Crowe picked on

George Cooley's spelling. "You have a perfect Spencerian hand, young man," he said.

George looked up at him hopefully.

"But your spelling is an abomination. What use are perfect letters if they are the wrong ones? Might as well put a new saddle on a cow, for all the good it'll do."

He tied Elmer Stone's left hand to his leg with a rag to keep him from writing with it. "It will be a great disadvantage to you to go out into the world writing left-handed," Professor Crowe told him. "People will take notice, and you will have a disadvantage in your affairs. You will use only your right hand from now on."

Poor Elmer struggled to write with his right hand, but his writing came out so squiggly that Professor Crowe made him do his work over and over until Elmer nearly cried.

It was all Rose could do to stay inside that room. The only thing that kept her from jumping up and leaving were the sour looks she exchanged with the other children. They all hated Professor Crowe, and in hating him, they had all become friends.

The Stove Prank

"I don't want to hear that sort of talk in this house," Mama scolded as she bustled about the kitchen getting supper. "Put a few sticks of wood in the stove while I check the rabbit stew."

"But Mama, he really is hateful. I can't help it. All the children . . . don't like him," Rose said, trying not to use the word "hate" again. She picked out four sticks of wood from the woodbox, opened the firebox door, and tucked them into the hissing red coals. She basked for a moment in the soothing warmth.

Papa's heavy steps sounded on the porch

outside, and then came the scraping noises of his cleaning the mud from his shoes. Rose set the plates on the table and cleared a place for the bread platter and the bowl of kraut that Mama had fried in drippings.

Then Papa came in and washed his hands in the pan by the door. He combed his hair in the little mirror that hung on the wall above it.

"He's mean when he talks," Rose persisted. "And he tied Elmer Stone's hand so he could hardly write, and he told George Cooley he was no better'n a cow! I can't bear him!"

"You can if I say you can," Mama warned, dishing up the stew. The smell of the good food made Rose extra glad to be home.

"What's all this about, now?" asked Papa as he sat down to eat.

Rose overflowed with her earnest complaints, until Mama finally shushed her. "That's enough. Be still and eat your supper."

They ate in silence for a few moments. The delicious dark bits of rabbit melted in Rose's mouth, and she sopped up the savory juice with a piece of cornbread. But she thought

Mama did not understand, and she sighed from trying to make her see.

Finally Mama put down her fork and spoke. "I once had a teacher I didn't like. She was very mean and unfair, especially to your aunt Carrie, who was very small and sickly. Do you know what your grandpa Ingalls told me?"

"What?"

"He said Teacher may have been wrong, but she was the teacher and I must mind her, no matter what I thought. Hard as it was for me to be good, that is what I did, even when everyone else in school was disobedient. What cannot be cured, must be endured. How will you get along in life if you complain every time you come across someone you don't like?"

Rose sighed and stared at her plate.

"Hmmpff!" Papa chortled. He got up, opened the door, and threw a rabbit bone out on the porch for Fido.

"What do you find so amusing?" Mama asked.

"I was just thinking," said Papa. "I seem to remember you causing that teacher a world of mischief. Didn't you practically move the whole school off its foundation one day, rocking in your seat?"

"Well, not exactly," Mama said, blinking fast. "I was very young, and . . . and strong willed. Too much so for my own good. But Ma and Pa set me right about it. I mean for Rose to have the same lesson."

"What does Pa mean, 'rocked the whole school'?" Rose wanted to know.

"Never mind about that," said Mama quickly. "It was just a childish prank a long time ago. Professor Crowe may not be the sort of teacher you would like, but if you pay attention to your lessons and mind your manners, I'm sure there'll be no trouble. Besides, it's only the first day. It is perfectly natural for a new teacher to begin by being strict."

"I heard he's a pretty rough fellow," said Papa, dishing up seconds of the kraut. "One of the men at Young's livery stable said he knew of him in Springfield. Crowe taught in a school there and got into a fistfight with a big boy. Knocked out two of his front teeth."

Rose was shocked. A teacher in a fistfight with a boy! She couldn't imagine it.

Mama looked at Papa thoughtfully for a moment. Then she speared a piece of rabbit meat and said, "I don't hold with gossip. And everyone deserves another chance."

The next morning Rose awoke feeling a mix of dread and excitement. She didn't want to go through another day at school like the first. She had heard some of the boys whispering that they would play a trick on Professor Crowe. She wanted to see if they would, and what it might be.

For the first time she could remember, Rose was early for school. The day had dawned bright, sunny, and bitter cold. Two boys struggled up the stairs with armfuls of extra wood for the heating stove. After they piled the wood on the floor, Rose noticed them nudging the stove sideways a little with their feet, looking up at the long stovepipe that went into the ceiling, and giggling. But she didn't understand why.

Rose helped Cora Hibbard haul buckets of water from the spring on the other side of the road for drinking and for heating on the stove.

Then Professor Crowe arrived, clomping heavily up the stairs. "Hurry, it's Teacher!" someone hissed, and everyone jumped into their seats.

Without a word he went to the cloakroom, took off his coat, and then went to his desk, his cane switch in his hand. He rang the bell to take up books, and everyone quietly opened their readers.

"We will begin today with recitation on page twenty-five, the story 'Perseverance.'" They took turns reading paragraphs from a dull story about a boy and girl trying to fly a kite.

Gusts of wind rattled the big windows, and the pot of hot water hissed on the heating stove in the back of the room. The voices droned on and on. Professor Crowe corrected the scholars' articulation in a mocking voice.

"The word is a-*gain*, Mr. Eagers," Professor Crowe said peevishly. "Not a-gin. You have eyes in your head, don't you, boy? Then open them and look at the letters of the words before you say them."

Rose grew more and more bored. She stared out the window at the tops of the trees flailing in the cold wind. Then she spotted Oscar Hensley making faces at George Cooley.

Oscar had hardly any bone in his nose. He could mash it almost flat against his face with his thumb. It was comical to see him do it, and George's face flushed bright red from trying not to laugh. Then he could not hold back anymore and guffawed loudly.

Professor Crowe sprang to his feet. His eyebrows arched wickedly as he searched the boys' side of the room. Then he spied George's red face. He strode over without a word, grabbed George's arm, and dragged him to the front of the room.

"Let this be an example to all of you," Professor Crowe declared. Then he whipped George across the shoulders with his cane switch. He struck George six times, and each time every shoulder in the room hunched as if it too had been struck and stung with pain.

George winced and grunted, but wouldn't let himself cry out. On the last blow, Professor Crowe hit George so hard that a piece of his switch broke off and flew across the room.

Then George sat down, his head bent, snuffling quietly. A cramp began to clench Rose's stomach. It scared her to see a grown-up hit a child. She couldn't remember Mama ever even spanking her. She had seen teachers use a ruler to beat a boy's palms, or make a mischievous boy stand with his nose to the chalkboard. But she had never had a teacher who was so rough. It made her angry and scared and sad all at the same time.

Finally it was time for recess. On their way to the cloakroom, some of the boys stopped by the stove to warm their hands. They slyly kicked at the stove's feet, and it skidded just a bit. The stovepipe was beginning to tilt a little.

On the girls' playground, the Fourth Reader girls stood in a knot, their hands tucked under their arms for warmth, gossiping.

"I had a worse teacher than him," Lula Faddis said. "He horsewhipped a big boy once.

My pa says you got to have a strict teacher to take on some of them bad boys. If my brothers got a whipping at school, he whipped 'em again when they come home."

"Teacher hadn't any need to whip George," Rose declared. "He's just plain mean."

"We begged Mama not to make us come back to school," Dora Hibbard said, jumping up and down to warm herself. "But she said we must. Oh, I just wish we could have Miss Pimberton back."

"My papa's on the school committee," said Blanche. "He says Miss Pimberton up and married and the committee couldn't find another teacher so soon. He said we must be good as we can and endure it. But I don't know how I can."

When the bell rang to call the children back to books, Rose found the Fourth Reader boys huddled by the front door, whispering and giggling. Just before she reached the door, they all rushed inside.

She followed them up the stairs, and as she walked into the classroom, she saw them each pass by the stove, giving it another kick. The last one, Jess Robinett, gave it a hard poke. Then he jumped out of the way just as the stovepipe pulled loose from the ceiling. The whole pipe began to lean.

"Look out!" Rose shouted. Then it fell to the floor with a crash and a great clattering. A cloud of black dust exploded from the top end of the pipe. The bottom end came off the stove, and a billow of smoke and sparks rose from the open vent toward the ceiling.

One of the girls screamed. The boys burst out in nervous laughter.

"What in tarnation?" Professor Crowe growled. He marched on clomping shoes to the stove. The children milled about, confused and scared, looking at each other with questioning eyes. Professor Curty, who taught the Fifth and Sixth Readers across the hall, poked his head in.

"Everyone all right in here?" he asked.

"I believe so," said Professor Crowe with a dark scowl. "Looks like the pipe worked itself loose. I expect I'll have to cancel lessons 'til it can be fixed."

Professor Crowe looked at the stove and kicked at the pipe. Then he stooped to look at something on the floor. He put his finger on a spot on the floor, where one of the stove feet had sat. The wood was brighter there.

Then Professor Crowe stood up slowly, turned, and looked around the room at all the students. His face flushed red. His eyes narrowed. Two veins on his forehead pushed themselves out like horns. Everyone shrank back a step. His mustache quivered for a moment, and then he barked, "Who called out? Who witnessed the perpetration of this outrage?"

All the children looked at one another and shrugged, except Rose. She felt fluttery in her chest, and her breath came in shallow gulps. She stared at the floor, but she felt the sidelong glances of Lula and Blanche and Lydia.

Professor Crowe raised his cane switch and stepped toward the middle of the room. Everyone shrank back another step.

"I said, who called out?" he roared. "Who shouted, 'Look out?' "

Rose dared not speak. Her legs tingled with fear, and her neck flushed hot. The room was deathly quiet, except for the rattling windows, and the muffled sound of voices from the other rooms. Smoke from the stove swirled against the ceiling.

Professor Crowe's eyes flashed, and he slammed the cane switch down on the top of the nearest desk—*WHACK!* Everyone flinched.

"Very well," he sneered. "As none of you are willing to step forward and name the party responsible for moving the stove so the pipe would fall, you will all be punished. Every last one of you will stay in and do your lessons during recess, for the entire session! Now you may as well go to your homes. We will take up books again in the morning when the pipe has been repaired."

Rose's stomach churned as she went to the cloakroom and got her coat and hat and mittens.

"Are you going to tell?" Blanche whispered in her ear.

"No," Rose said. "Why should I?" She took down her coat and hat and went to stand with

Blanche in the corner, away from the other scholars so they couldn't hear.

"But then we'll all be punished," Blanche whined. "It isn't fair to punish everyone."

"It's none of my doing," Rose said. She remembered the time Paul Cooley's father had punished him for something he didn't do. It was Rose's fault, but Paul wouldn't tell on her, not even to save himself. Rose could be just as brave as any boy.

"I wouldn't tell even if he beat me with his old stick," she said proudly. "I just wouldn't. It isn't for me to tell. It's for those boys to say who did it."

Blanche made a face. "I expect so," she said with a sigh. "But none of them ever will, and it will only get worse. I have three brothers, and I know how horrid those boys can be."

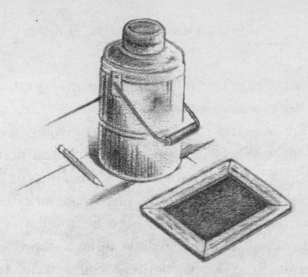

The Last Straw

The next day the boys tried to be as good as they could. No one made any funny faces, and there were no tricks played. At recess Professor Crowe made everyone stay inside and continue their lessons. The only time they could relax was when teacher left the room. Then everyone's shoulders sagged; their sighs sounded like snow sliding off a roof.

"He can't keep us in forever," George Cooley told Rose in the cloakroom on his way home. "He has to give up sometime."

But Professor Crowe meant to keep his

word. There was no recess the next day either.

Rose was miserable. Without any recess there was no time to visit and play with Blanche. She would sooner have stayed home and studied her lessons with Mama, but Mama wouldn't hear of it. "You must make an effort, and not quit at the first sign of trouble," she told Rose. "Patience will wear out a stone."

But Rose knew nothing could wear the meanness out of Professor Crowe.

Friday came, the day of the weekly spell-down. Rose had almost always won the spelldowns in the Third Reader, so she wasn't the least bit nervous.

She stayed in during dinnertime, eating at her desk, and then reading some more in *Gulliver's Travels*. All the other students went outside to play games, or walked to their homes to eat with their families.

Before the end of the dinner hour, before Professor Crowe came back from eating his own dinner at the boardinghouse, Jess Robinett walked into the quiet classroom and looked around. He seemed as skittish as a sparrow.

"Is Teacher back yet?" he whispered to Rose. He was clutching his coat. Something bulged in there.

"No," Rose said.

Then Jess opened his coat. Inside it he had a raccoon pelt. He dashed out and clumped back down the stairs. Rose followed him, out into the second floor hallway. Jess was at the bottom of the stairs. He took the pelt and dragged it along the floor of the foyer, and then up the stairs, making sure it had swiped each stair step.

He huffed his way up the stairs, the pelt touching every step. Then he dragged it into the classroom, all around the floor along the walls, and then into the cloakroom.

Rose followed him, gaping.

"What are you doing?" She knew it was some kind of trick, but she couldn't imagine what it could be.

"Just you be quiet about it," he snarled. "You'll find out soon enough." Then he stuffed the pelt into the sleeve of his coat and hung it up on a peg.

When lessons took up, Rose could hardly concentrate, wondering about the trick and when it would be played. Jess kept his shaggy head down and sneaked a sidelong look at Rose now and then. He grinned, his face turned crimson, and his long, feathery cowlick trembled with silent laughing.

Finally Professor Crowe said it was time for the spelldown. All the children got up and stood on the line of chalk that Professor Crowe had drawn along one side of the room, by the windows. He sat at his desk, reading out the words from his spelling book and listening as the scholars spelled.

After the first few children had been spelled down, Rose heard dogs barking somewhere down the hill in town. It was the same sort of barking and howling that she had heard late at night, lying in her bed. Those were the voices of hunting dogs—raccoon-hunting dogs.

Professor Crowe had just given Rose a word to spell, *fragrance*, when Jess raised his hand, with his index finger poking up. He was biting his lower lip.

"*Fragrance*," Rose repeated. "F-r-a *fra*, g-r-a-n-c-e *grance*. Fragrance."

"Yes?" Professor Crowe said, peering at Jess over his spectacles. "I see. I'm sure you can wait a bit longer, until the spelldown is over."

"Gee whillikins, Teacher," Jess pleaded, squirming and hopping from foot to foot. "I got to go. Honest."

"Oh, well, go on then," Professor Crowe said, dismissing Jess with a disgusted wave of his hand. "Next scholar, then. The word is *instruction*."

Rose watched in fascination as Jess raced into the cloakroom. He took an extra long time in there getting his coat. Then he raced out of the cloakroom and down the stairs. Rose noticed that he had left the door ajar.

Professor Crowe gave three more scholars their words, and two of them made mistakes and had to sit down. Suddenly the sound of dogs howling and barking broke out nearby. All the children craned to look out the windows. The line of spellers became ragged. Two boys who had been spelled down stood up to see better.

"In your places!" Professor Crowe demanded. Then there was a loud commotion in the stairway, and the sound exploded inside, with those dogs barking and their wild, bloodthirsty howls. The school echoed with the hollow pounding of paws and the scrabbling of claws on the stair steps. A wave of nervous giggling broke out among the scholars.

Professor Crowe stood up and tore off his spectacles. "What the dickens is it now?" he said roughly. He strode to the door on his long legs. He reached out to to grab the handle when it burst open on its own. In flew the long, lean body of a brown-and-black hunting dog, its ears flopping, its face grinning, and its tongue lolling. The dog's front paws landed right on Professor Crowe's chest. He went down with a thud.

Rose shrieked. More dogs poured in through the door—six in all—trampling right over Professor Crowe. His arms and legs waved wildly in the air as he tried to fight them off and get up. Now all the children were scream-ing and laughing. The dogs howled, whined, barked, and snarled at one another as they raced around the room, their noses to the floor.

Children flew in every direction. Desks tipped over and hit the floor with loud bangs. Blanche backed into a corner and huddled there. Lula hunched by a turned-over desk. Rose ran to a window and climbed up on the sill.

Professor Crowe stood up and swore. He brushed his pants and kicked at one of the baying dogs. His bow tie was undone, his celluloid collar was gone, and his jacket, pants, and shirt were covered with muddy paw prints.

Professor Curty came running from across the hallway.

"What in heaven's name!" he shouted.

Then one of the dogs, the first one that had knocked down Professor Crowe, raised its head and set up a fearful new howling. It darted into the cloakroom. All the other dogs followed, and a fresh squall of snarling broke out in there. The dogs were fighting.

Now all the teachers in the school had come to the door, their eyes wide and frightened. A cluster of children from the other readers peered from behind.

"It's some devilment by these no-account youngsters!" Professor Crowe shouted, waving his arm at the room. "I knew I should never have come to this vile backwater! Bunch of untamed savages!"

Now the dogs burst out of the cloakroom. Two of them were growling deeply and tugging at a long black coat. With each pull the cloth made a sickening ripping sound. Then they were all snapping at it, trying to steal it away from the others. The noise was terrifying.

Professor Crowe's eyes popped, and his jaw dropped. "My coat!" he shrieked. "The filthy varmints have got my coat!"

Suddenly, out of one of the torn sleeves, the leader dog snatched the raccoon pelt. He dashed out the door between the legs of the teachers and students. Rose could hear the dog bounding down the stairs. All the other dogs followed, howling and snapping as they went, knocking down some of the screaming children as they bolted out the door.

Professor Crowe reached down and picked up his tattered coat. A sleeve was completely torn off. The back hung in shreds. Professor Curty and the other teachers shifted restlessly.

"Now, I'm sorry about this, Crowe," Professor Curty finally said, wringing his hands. "These boys get a little coltish now and again, but I'm sure no real harm was meant by it."

"Hunh!" Professor Crowe barked. The Fourth Reader scholars all backed up into the far corner, as far from him as they could get. Rose climbed down from the windowsill and went to stand next to Blanche.

Professor Crowe looked around the room. The veins in his forehead and his neck stood out, and his face blazed bright red. Then he exploded.

"A bunch of good-for-nothing heathens!" he sputtered shaking his fist. "This is how you treat a man of culture? This is your opinion of learning? Why, you're nothing more than a mob of miserable, shiftless, animals! I wouldn't give a nickel for the lot of you."

Then he whirled to face the teachers standing in the doorway. "This is the last straw, Curty! The school committee will pay for this damage, and my fare back to Springfield. I won't spend another day in this godforsaken place! Good day and good riddance!"

Then he stomped out, pushing his way through the crowd, dragging the torn coat after him.

A Useful Lesson

Rose did not snitch on Jess Robinett. But everyone in town knew he was the one who tricked Professor Crowe. His big brother had borrowed the hunting dogs from a farmer and then bragged at the livery stable and at Reynolds' store about helping Jess run Teacher out of town.

By the time Rose and Spookendyke got home from school, Papa had already heard about it from Abe. Abe had been at the hotel delivering a wagonload of stovewood when Professor Crowe stormed in with his ruined coat.

Papa met Rose coming up the hill from

the new bridge across Fry Creek, where Fido always greeted her with joyful yelps. Papa's brown eyes were bright, and his mustache quivered with mirth.

"I want to hear every word," he said eagerly, "before we go in the house. Your Mama . . . well . . ."

"I know," Rose said. "She doesn't like a mean-spirited trick. But Professor Crowe was mean, too, Papa."

He took Spookendyke's reins and led the donkey up the hill into the barnyard. He helped Rose put away the saddle, settle the donkey in his stall, and fill his trough with oats.

"Come with me to the dairy barn," Papa said, looking over his shoulder at the house. "You can tell me all about it while I milk."

So Rose perched on a block of wood while Papa sat milking in the cozy barn, his head leaning against Bunting's flank. Her calf, Spark, stuck his head between the stall rails and bawled for a drink. The dairy barn stayed nice and warm from the heat of the animals.

"I'll be starched!" Papa exclaimed when Rose

told how Jess had used the raccoon pelt to lure the dogs to the schoolhouse. Then he roared with laughter when she told how the dogs knocked Professor Crowe down, and then tore his coat to shreds. Papa's guffaws startled Bunting and she nearly kicked over the milk pail. Rose couldn't help giggling along with him.

Papa was still chuckling when the door creaked open and Mama stepped inside.

"What's so humorous?" she asked. Papa burst out laughing again. He looked at Rose and shrugged.

"Might as well tell her," he said. "She'll hear about it anyway."

So Rose repeated the story, while Bunting's milk streamed foaming and singing into the pail. Mama frowned with disapproval at first. "Land sakes!" she exclaimed, and "Gracious! What a terrible thing to do to a body."

But her mouth wobbled a bit when Papa began to laugh again. And finally she let herself go and laughed as hard as Rose had ever seen her. Even Spark seemed to enjoy the joke, dancing around his little stall and bawling.

"Oh, my!" Mama said when she'd got her breath back. "I can hardly wait to write about this to Pa. He always likes a good story."

Professor Crowe did leave town, that very night. Abe said Mr. Robinett gave Jess a good licking, but Jess didn't mind because all the boys and men in town treated him like a hero.

Now there was no teacher for the Fourth Reader. Mama said classes might be canceled for the whole session. Rose wasn't sure whether to feel glad or not. It had been something new, the way the children came together against Professor Crowe.

But then, on Sunday at church, Professor Curty announced that the school committee had a found a teacher to take Professor Crowe's place. It was none other than Miss Pimberton! Except now she was to be called Mrs. Honeycutt, because she had married Eldon Honeycutt, an engineer for the railroad.

Rose chirped so loud with joy that Mama had to scold her.

After that Rose looked forward to every day of school. Mrs. Honeycutt was the best teacher

Rose had ever had. She led the class in singing and taught them play-party games. She read wonderful stories to them from books, and played Crack-the-Whip with them at recess, laughing as hard as any of them when she fell down. She was gentle and patient and always had a smile. Even the boys obeyed her.

She was very clever, too. One day, when Rose went to the cloakroom to get her coat to go out for afternoon recess and play in the new snowfall, she couldn't find her tam o' shanter. Hot tears blurred her eyes as she searched frantically among the other coats, on the floor, even on the shelf of dinner pails. But it wasn't anywhere to be found. She just knew someone had taken it!

"Now, now. Don't fret," Mrs. Honeycutt said. "I'm sure it will turn up." She took her own fascinator and tied it around Rose's head. "There! Now go and play, and we will see what's to be done about it after recess."

"Thank you, ma'am," Rose said with a wobble in her voice and a lump in her throat. She could not believe that she would ever see her beautiful hat again. She was miserable during recess. She stood and watched the other children throwing snowballs and making snow angels, wondering all the while how she could ever face Mama and tell her that the hat was gone.

Then she noticed Mrs. Honeycutt come out of the schoolhouse. She walked a little way into the woods, and seemed to be looking for something on the ground.

When the bell rang to take up books again, Mrs. Honeycutt came back, holding a small branch in her hand that was shaped like the letter T.

Rose carefully put the fascinator back on Mrs. Honeycutt's hook. After everyone had hung up their hats and coats and settled in their desks, Mrs. Honeycutt stood before the class, holding the stick in her hand. Her face was set and her mouth was pursed. The scholars looked at one another in wonderment. She never whipped anyone, not even Harry Carnall when he tied Ida Goss's pinafore to her chair. But it looked like she meant to whip someone with that stick.

"I'm very sorry to say that it seems someone in this room may have taken the hat of another scholar," she said. Every head wagged like a startled chicken's, as they looked at one another to see if they could tell whose hat was taken. Rose squinched down in her seat.

"It is a blue tam o' shanter, belonging to Rose Wilder."

Blanche gasped and looked at Rose. Then every eye was on her. Rose stared at her desk top and her neck burned hot.

"Perhaps this was a mistake," Mrs. Honeycutt said in a firm voice. "But in case it was not, I have collected this stick in the woods," she said, holding it up to show to the class. "It is a known fact that a hickory branch in the shape of a T can find a thief. If I throw it in the air, it will land on the top of the head of the person who took the hat.

"If someone did take the hat, or knows of its whereabouts, he or she should speak now, and all will be forgiven."

A nervous titter ran through the room as everyone twisted and turned in their seats, looking for the thief to stand up and confess. But no one did.

"Very well, then," Mrs. Honeycutt said. "We will let the stick tell us if the hat was truly stolen." She waved that stick and drew her arm back to throw it. Suddenly Lula Faddis shouted out, "Almeda done it! She dodged, Teacher. I seen her."

"Yes, I saw," said Mrs. Honeycutt.

She walked down the rows of desks to where Almeda Fike was sitting, a miserable look on her crimson face, her stringy unbraided hair trembling. Almeda was one of the poor country girls who came to school with no hat or fascinator to keep her head warm in the bitter cold.

Rose's heart ached to see her slumped in her seat, quaking like a trapped animal. Almeda had ducked when Mrs. Honeycutt started to throw the stick. She was the only one who did. She had given herself away.

Mrs. Honeycutt put her hand on Almeda's shoulder. She said gently, "Almeda, do you know where Rose's hat is?"

Poor Almeda stared at her desk and silently

nodded. A tear fell from her cheek.

"Where is it, dear?"

Almeda mumbled some words that Rose couldn't hear.

"Children, I will return presently. Please remain in your seats, and study your ciphering lessons."

Mrs. Honeycutt and Almeda put on their warm things and walked out of the room and down the stairs. As soon as they heard the front door of the school close, everyone jumped up from their desks and ran to the windows.

"There they are!" Harry Carnall shouted from the back. Rose ran and peered out through the wavy glass. Mrs. Honeycutt walked with Almeda through the snow to the edge of the girls' playground, to an old log that lay on the ground. Almeda kicked away some snow, reached down, and picked up the tam o' shanter. Rose breathed a big sigh of relief.

Mrs. Honeycutt took the tam o' shanter and brushed off the snow. Then she squatted down, took off her fascinator, and tied it around Almeda's head, tucking the ends into her threadbare coat. Her breath came in puffs of steam; she was speaking to Almeda. Almeda wiped her eyes. Then Mrs. Honeycutt hugged Almeda, patted her on the shoulder, and sent her to the horse shed.

Mrs. Honeycutt watched Almeda untether her mule, climb up on it, and ride off. Then she turned back toward the schoolhouse, holding Rose's hat in her hand.

The children scrambled back to their seats, got out their slates, bent their heads, and began scribbling their numbers, stealing glances at Rose and one another. Everyone wondered what was to become of Almeda.

Mrs. Honeycutt came back, took off her coat in the cloakroom, and stood by the heater stove warming herself.

"Rose's hat is back where it belongs," she finally said, rubbing her hands together. "And I have sent Almeda home for the day. She knows she has made a mistake and she is very sorry for it. Everyone makes a mistake from time to time. We must remember that they who forgive most will be most forgiven.

"When Almeda returns to school, no one will tease her or I promise they will be punished. Now, let us begin our ciphering lessons."

Rose looked at Mrs. Honeycutt with a brimming heart. She knew that no one could ever be more kind or fair.

When Teacher had rung the bell to end that day's lessons, Rose dawdled in the cloakroom pulling on her coat and putting on her beloved tam o' shanter. Finally, when all the other children had left, she walked up to Teacher's desk.

"Thank you ever so much, Mrs. Honeycutt."

"You are most welcome, Rose," she answered, putting down her pen and smiling.

Rose stood there, thinking and looking at the hickory branch lying on the corner of the desk.

"What is it?" Mrs. Honeycutt finally asked.

"Is it really true, about the stick knowing who is a thief?"

Mrs. Honeycutt put the cap on her beautiful fountain pen with a little *snap* and began to gather up her books. "What do *you* think?" she asked, a twinkle in her eye.

Rose thought a moment. "I think only a thief would think it is true."

Mrs. Honeycutt beamed. "Then you have learned a useful lesson, Rose."

The Wish Book

It snowed a little bit every few days in the weeks before Christmas. Those were pleasant snowstorms without much wind. The flakes fell thick and soft as goose down, and then the sun came out strong and bright on the days in between to take the bite out of the frosty air.

On some days Rose left Spookendyke in his warm stall and dragged her sled to school. At recess and dinnertime she rode it down the big, big hill that sloped toward town, and she slid down Patterson's Hill on the way home. She shared rides with Blanche and Lula and Lydia.

Even Mrs. Honeycutt took a slide. Her skirt flew up, and she shrieked as loudly as any of them.

On Sundays after church, Swiney came to visit dragging his own sled that Papa had made last Christmas. Papa had built that sled for Rose. But she had decided, with Papa, that he ought to give it to Swiney instead, from Santa Claus, because Abe had nothing to give him.

After that, Papa had built another sled for Rose. But it had scarcely snowed enough last winter to play with it. Now, with the ground heaped with snow as soft and fluffy as scoops of beaten potatoes, she and Swiney raced each other down the hill toward Fry Creek, Fido chasing after with excited barks.

Now Papa worked in the barn each afternoon, building something for Mama and Rose for Christmas. On the frosty nights, he sat by the kitchen stove whittling a toy pistol out of a piece of wood for Swiney, and a wooden ladle for Effie. He blackened the toy pistol with boot polish, and rubbed the ladle with linseed oil 'til it gleamed in the firelight.

Rose and Mama sat together in front of the cozy fireplace knitting mittens and fascinators and warm woolen stockings, embroidering muslin handkerchiefs, tatting lace for collars, and sewing up shirts out of new chambray.

Rose found snatches of time—when Mama went to town with Papa to Reynolds' store, or went visiting to Abe and Effie's—to sew up a new apron for Mama out of scraps from the scrap bag.

On the last day of school before Christmas, Mrs. Honeycutt brought a big bag of candy for all the children, and sent them all to their homes singing carols. On Christmas Eve after church, Rose and Mama made popcorn balls to give to the serenaders who came by shooting off their guns and ringing cowbells.

Abe and Effie and Swiney stayed for oyster stew, and then they exchanged presents. The house filled with oohs and aahs of delight. Papa had made Mama a beautiful whatnot shelf for the corner. Now Mama had a place to show off her keepsakes, like the tiny ceramic jewel box with the wee ceramic tea setting on top that she had gotten for Christmas when she was a little girl.

Papa had made Rose a beautiful small chest of drawers with shiny white porcelain knobs. Now she would have a place to keep her stockings and underclothes, her Christmas pennies and the nickel she saved from Fourth of July, the cornshuck doll that Abe had made for her last fall, and the arrowheads she had found along the creek. She couldn't stop sliding the drawers open and shut, thinking what to put in each one.

On Christmas morning, Mama spoiled the hens with corn in their mash. Fido got a whole hambone to chew on. Mama gave Blackfoot the heart and gizzard from a hen she had cooked, and the horses and mules each got a Christmas apple. Then Rose and Swiney dragged their sleds over to Alva's house to play. They hunted for redbirds, and saw three. Seeing a redbird on Christmas Day was an omen of good luck.

It was a wonderful, rich Christmas, the best that Rose could remember. The only thing missing was Grandma and Grandpa Ingalls and her aunts, Mary, Carrie, and Grace. This was the third Christmas since the Wilders had left the family behind in South Dakota.

But there were the letters and gifts they had sent—Rose's blind aunt Mary had made her a rag doll out of cotton batting—and the good memories of Christmases past that Mama told about in stories around the fireplace or the kitchen table.

One warm, breezy Saturday morning during the January thaw, Papa drove the empty wagon to town to help the Cooleys move from the hotel into their new house. Mr. Cooley worked for the railroad now. George and Paul could be boys like other boys, playing after school and visiting on Sundays instead of working every spare minute in the hotel. And Mrs. Cooley had her parlor.

After Papa came home, and he had stabled and fed the team, he came into the kitchen with a big, thick book under his arm. Rose sat in a chair, pumping the dash up and down in the butter churn. Mama stood ironing one of Papa's shirts on the kitchen table. Papa walked over and without a word dropped the book on the table, in front of Mama. It landed with a loud *thump!*

Mama peered at the cover. "What is this?" she asked, pressing hard at the collar and trying to read at the same time. Rose dropped the dash and got up to look.

The cover of that book was a riot of colors and pictures and words. A fat man with white hair and rosy cheeks, dressed in a flowing tunic, sat beside a great horn of plenty bursting with all sorts of made things: a piano, a stove, furniture. In the distance was a picture of rich fields of green corn and golden wheat.

At the top of the cover was a picture of the earth with deep-blue oceans and puffy white clouds swirling around and words. Rose read them aloud: " '*The Consumers' Guide*. Sears, Roebuck and Company, Cheapest Supply House on Earth. The Most Pro- . . . Progressive Concern of Its Kind in the World.' What does it mean, 'progressive'?"

160

"Forward-looking," said Mama. "What is this about, Manly? Whose book is it?"

"It's ours," said Papa, hanging his coat on a peg by the door. "Cooley gave it to me. Some drummer left it behind in the hotel. It's the new way of trading, Bess. Wait 'til you see what's inside. It's got everything a body could ever need or want, from cradle to grave. Just look."

Mama set the flatiron on the stove, hung up Papa's shirt, and they all sat down. Mama and Rose scrunched their chairs close on either side of Papa, to look at that book.

"Folks call it a wish book," Papa explained, his voice bright and chirpy. "You see what you want, and mail the company a letter with the money to pay for it. They send it to you by the mail, or express. The best part is . . . look, it says right here," he said excitedly, turning some pages, "the prices are nearly wholesale. Why some of 'em are half what Reynolds gets!"

He flipped through the pages quickly. "They've got a whole set of harness in here that's just fourteen dollars. These Sears,

Roebuck people are going to put the town merchants right out of business."

Every page was full of pictures and words and prices, so much to look at that Rose's eyes ached from stretching to see them all. Papa was searching for the harnesses when the book fell open to a page of ladies' drawers and corsets, and pictures of women wearing them, their arms and ankles shockingly bare.

Rose couldn't stifle a giggle.

"Oops!" Papa said, blushing and quickly flipping past. "Sorry, Bess."

"Land sakes," said Mama, putting a hand to her chest. "It's shameful the things they put into print nowadays. Right out in plain view for men to see. Rose, the butter's not going to come just sitting there. You can churn and look at the same time."

Rose grumbled to herself as she dragged the churn over by the table. She could hardly tear herself away for even an instant. She grabbed the end of the dash and began the *slop-slop* rhythm of the churn again, looking over the huddled shoulders of Mama and Papa.

"These new shirtwaists are lovely," said Mama. "And for fifty cents, why I could hardly sew one up for less at the prices Reynolds gets for percale, if he even has it in. But you'd have to starve yourself to look like the girls in this picture."

The ladies in that drawing had impossibly tiny waists. But Rose thought Mama would look just beautiful in one, with its soft, billowy leg-o'-mutton shoulders, and crisp linen collar and cuffs.

It was true, what Papa had said: There was everything in the world anyone could wish for, right there in that book. There were beautiful dresses for women, and even for little girls.

"Oh, Mama, look at that one!" Rose cried out. It was a girl's sailor suit, with leg-o'-mutton sleeves and striped collar and cuffs, and stripes across the chest.

"It's very cunning," Mama said. "I could try to make one, but it looks hard to sew up, with all that fancy braid."

The little girl wearing that dress had her hair

beautifully curled and fluffed up. It covered her ears and almost touched her cheeks. She looked like a little lamb. Rose couldn't take her eyes from that drawing. She could nearly hear the whispering rustle of the pillowy sleeves and imagine herself with the same lovely hair as that girl.

Then Mama flipped some more pages. She was flipping too fast. Rose wanted to look at one page and see and read everything on it before she went to the next, the way she read a storybook. Seeing all those pictures fly by was confusing.

There were pictures of autoharps and kraut cutters and mechanical pencils and boys' fedora hats and a wonderful thing called a bicycle for riding, and stoves and even whole wagons and buggies.

"Look at this, Bess. A fruit dryer," Papa pointed out. "Says here you can dry five bushels of fruit in it in a single day. Jiminy, when the orchard comes into bearing, we could use a machine like that. Think of all the falls we could save that'd just rot or have to go into the cider press. Why, that dryer could pay for itself in a couple of seasons."

Just then, Bunting's loudest bellow came echoing from the dairy barn.

"Golly!" Papa cried, jumping up and fumbling for his pocket watch. "Look where the time went. I've got to get the stock fed and the cows milked." Then he grabbed his hat from its peg on the wall and dashed out the door.

"And I have to put up this ironing and fix supper," Mama said, closing the book and standing up. "We've wasted enough time as it is." She set it on a shelf. Rose gazed wistfully at it as she hurried to get the butter all churned.

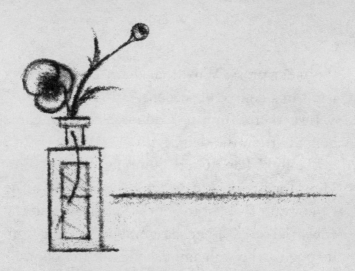

A Good Many Tricks

All the next week, every chance and stolen moment they could find, Mama, Papa, and Rose pored over the wish book. Mama said it was an encyclopedia of modern civilization. Papa said it was a sign of the coming greatness of the country.

"The little man's been under the thumb of the merchants for too long, Bess," said Papa. "Asking big prices and tacking on a big interest, to boot.

"Now they've got whole factories of machines that hardly need a man to run 'em, putting out goods that are cheaper to buy, and

166

all these new contraptions they've dreamed up for farming. That'll give us farmers more time to build up our land, and get a better crop."

"I wonder," Mama said thoughtfully, looking at a page of dress goods. "I don't like Reynolds' prices any better than the next person, or his liens. But without the merchants giving credit, a lot of farmers would have plain starved, including us, Manly. These Sears, Roebuck people don't give credit, and they don't give a hoot whether we eat or not. At least Mr. Reynolds knows he's going to have to look us in the face the next time we come up short.

"And who can tell from a picture if these items are of high quality or not? I would be afraid to buy dress goods I couldn't see and touch first."

Papa ran a hand over the axe handle he had whittled and was shaving smooth with a bit of broken glass. He gathered the little pile of shavings on the floor between his feet and tossed them into the cookstove.

"We've got some cash money laid by, Bess,"

he said, looking over Mama's shoulder. "There's a good many tricks you'd like to have in that book. Get what you want; they'll only cost a few cents."

"Well, all right," Mama said. "But only things we need."

So she spent a whole evening leafing through the wish book, writing down on one of her small notepads a list of things she might like to have. Rose sat at her elbow and helped her choose.

The first thing Rose wanted Mama to write down was a new hat. "That one is beautiful, Mama," Rose said. It was straw covered with ruffles and lace, and silk violets. It had a buckle on the front, a big bow that stood up on top, and a feather plume.

"Goodness, Rose." Mama chuckled. "You ought to look at the prices first. That hat is two dollars and two bits. I'd have to trade more than twenty dozen eggs just to pay for it."

Rose blushed. That *was* expensive. It would take Mama's hens three weeks to lay that many eggs.

But Mama did write down an untrimmed

straw hat that she thought would be nice to wear to church in summer. "It's just twenty-five cents and I can sew some ribbon on to dress it up," she said.

And she wrote down some dress goods that were cheaper than she could buy at Reynolds'. And a few yards of embroidery for dress cuffs and collars. She also wrote down:

> One doz. slate pencils @ 9¢
> One butter fork @ 15¢
> One gravy strainer @ 7¢
> One milk strainer @ 13¢
> One Porcelain Lined Cast Preserving
>   Kettle @ 55¢
> One doz. Stockinet Dress Shields
>   (sm.) @ 55¢
> One Egg sock darner @ 4¢
> One doz. safety pins, size 2½ @ 2½¢
> One doz. Polished rubber hair pins,
>   4¼ in. @ 30¢
> One whisk broom @ 5¢

The list seemed to go on forever. There

wasn't a page in that book that didn't have something they could use. It was a miracle that anyone could think up all those wonderful things.

And there were things for fun, too. There were stereoscopes, which were machines you could look into and see colored pictures that seemed almost real. Rose read aloud the descriptions of those pictures to Mama as she sat after supper darning socks: "parson carrying a pig, man swallowing rats, dentist drawing teeth."

"Who on earth would want to see a man swallowing a rat?" Mama chortled.

Rose especially liked to see the pages of books to buy. She read with longing the columns and columns of wonderful-sounding titles and authors' names: *A Connecticut Yankee in King Arthur's Court*, by Mark Twain; *Idle Thoughts of an Idle Fellow*, by Jerome K. Jerome; *Peck's Bad Boy and his Pa*; *Twice Told Tales*, by Nathaniel Hawthorne. There were storybooks for boys and storybooks for girls, books about locomotives, books of recitations and quotations, and books of poetry.

The Consumers' Guide said some books were

library editions, and were printed on calendered paper with covers of extra-silk-finish cloth, the title stamped in gold. How Rose wanted to hold and read every one of those books!"

"It would be lovely to have our own library of books," Mama agreed. "But we must mind our necessities first. Besides, you have books in school to read."

When Mama was done making the list, she let Rose add up the prices. It took her a long time, and she kept making mistakes. Arithmetic was Rose's hardest subject. When she was finally done, and had checked her figures, Rose was astonished. Not one thing that Mama picked out cost so very much money, but all together they added up to $6.42!

Mama sat down next to Rose, drying her hands on her apron. She took the pencil and began to scratch out some of the things on that list. But when she was done, the total was still more than four dollars.

"We'll put this away for now," she said, tucking the list inside the book. "It would be a terrible extravagance to throw away good money on frills when we're still paying off the mortgage and waiting for the orchard to come into bearing. Maybe when spring comes and we see how the hens are laying, and how crop conditions look."

Mama set aside some of her egg money each week, in a jar she kept on the fireplace mantel. Each week she let Rose add it up. The money grew very slowly. It was still winter, and the hens laid fewer eggs in the cold weather.

"Seems I remember them doing better last winter," Mama fretted. Even after three weeks, when Rose dumped the coins out on the table and counted them, there was only thirty-four cents in the jar.

"How could we ever pay for the things on that list?" Rose wondered.

"It takes a long time of scrimping and saving," said Mama. "We're farmers, not nabobs."

Then, after dinner on a warmish night in February, when the spring peepers had begun to sing for the first time, Mama put down her mending, got up from her rocker, and took down *The Consumers' Guide*.

Rose looked up hopefully from the letter she was writing to her aunt Mary. Mama pulled out the list, crumpled it up, and threw it into the cookstove fire.

Rose laid down her pencil and sighed. Her heart sank. She had wanted Mama to have a summer hat, and hairpins, and maybe even a shirtwaist.

"Why, Bess!" Papa exclaimed, a handful of popcorn stopped in midair between the bowl and his mouth. His newspaper slid off his lap to the floor. He dropped the popcorn back in the bowl and brushed off his hands.

"I thought we talked about that. A few dollars on notions won't break us. We've had a good year, and the future never looked better for us."

"I've thought about it and thought about it, and I realize I have all the things I need," Mama said firmly. "If Rose needs a slate pencil, I can trade for one at Reynolds' instead of paying good cash money for a dozen from some stranger in Chicago. I can pick out the lumps in my gravy with a spoon, the way I have all my life, and my mother and grandmother before me. I've got a perfectly good goose egg from Mrs. Stubbins for my sock darning, and I can keep using scraps of muslin for dress shields."

Papa grimaced and made a low grumbling sound in his throat. "Aw, Bess. A fella likes to spoil his best girl. But you won't hardly ever let me. What have we worked for all these years if we can't be a little foolish now and then?"

Mama put the book back on the shelf and came to Papa, settling in his lap. She took one of his hands in both of hers and smiled sweetly at him.

"You spoil me every day, with the flowers you bring in spring and summer, the furniture you make, the funny stories you tell about the folks in town, the walks we take in the woods. You spoil me in a thousand little ways that I would never be without." Mama bent down and gave Papa a good, long kiss.

Rose squirmed shyly in her chair and felt her face grow warm. When Mama sat back up, her eyes were bright and Papa was smiling.

"As for that list," Mama went on in a brisk

voice, "I have not missed a thing on it. But we would certainly miss the money to pay off Mr. Kinnebrew for the extra acres we bought, or to buy hay for the stock this summer in case of a dry spell, or for who knows what other needs might come up?"

Papa sighed, and Mama patted him on his head.

"I'm sorry, Manly. I know you mean well. But I learned a lesson from this wish book. The minute we think we need a thing, we begin paying for it whether we buy it or not."

Mama went back to her rocker and picked up her mending. Papa picked his newspaper up from the floor.

"Now my mind is clear," she said, laying a patch on a hole in the knee of Papa's overalls to see how to sew it. "I am content as a farm wife, making do with what we have until the farm is paid off. After all, it is the simple things in life that count, more than a whole world of fancy notions."

A Baby Is Coming!

Winter slowly relaxed its icy grip on the Ozarks. Gentle spring rains came to kiss the hills awake from their long slumber. At night as she lay in bed listening to the rain patter on the low roof just above her head, Rose heard the snarly growls of a bobcat out wandering the forest. The bobcat sounded angry. He cried ferociously, not caring if any hunter might hear him. But he wasn't angry. He was just lonely.

During the warming days, Effie came by to help turn and hoe the muddy garden one last time before planting, to clean out a fresh crop of rocks, and then to put in the peas and seed potatoes. The Wilders and the Bairds would eat from the same garden this year. Papa had plowed it in the fall, breaking some new ground for extra rows.

Every spring the garden sprouted a new crop of rocks. Every spring they cleaned the rocks out, but there were always more the next year. They had picked the perfect name for Rocky Ridge Farm.

This year, the rocks were buried in mud, and cleaning the muddy garden was a dirty job. The mud stuck to their shoes and made them heavy and hard to walk in. You couldn't work in that garden without getting mud on all of you, and getting soaked by rain. Mama had to rinse their dresses out every night.

"If I live to be a hundred I'll never see the end of rocks," Mama said, huffing as she flung a big one clattering onto the rock pile at the edge of the garden. She had smears of mud around both eyes, which made her look like a raccoon. "If Mr. Sears and Mr. Roebuck ever make a trade for rocks, we'll be rich as Midas."

The rock pile had grown and grown since the Wilders first moved to Rocky Ridge Farm. Now it was tall as a grown-up. Rose often scrambled over it playing King of the Mountain with Swiney and Alva.

One afternoon when they took a break from the gardening, Mama and Effie sat on the porch with their heads bent together, chatting quietly. Rose and Swiney went to the barn to see the new kittens that Blackfoot had hidden in the hayloft.

The children sat in the high doorway of the hayloft with their feet dangling down, cradling the tiny warm balls of fur in their hands one at a time. Blackfoot lay curled up on a nest of hay, purring softly as the kittens paddled her belly.

Rose gazed over the sodden, brown barnyard. Effie stood to stretch. She arched her back, and put her hands behind her hips. When she did that, her stomach made a soft mountain in her dress.

"Look how fat Effie's got." Rose giggled.

Swiney looked up from petting a kitten.

"She's not fat," he said. "She's got a baby coming."

Rose gasped. She looked at Swiney, and then back at Effie. She was just standing now, looking out on the swampy barnyard, but Rose could still see her fat belly gently pushing her dress out in front.

Then it hit her like a thunderclap. A jolt of excitement ran all along her legs and arms and she would have shrieked with joy except she didn't dare with Effie close enough to hear.

A baby was coming! A baby was *really* coming!

"When?" Rose whispered, breathless with excitement.

"Dunno," said Swiney, holding the kitten against his cheek. "Whenever the granny woman comes to bring it. Cats and cows and pigs and even horses have 'em in the spring. Maybe it'll be soon now."

"But I was born in December," Rose wailed. "Oh, I hope it isn't that long to wait! I couldn't bear it. Isn't it wonderful! You'll be a . . . an uncle!"

Swiney just shrugged. He didn't love babies the way Rose did. No one could love babies as much as she. And when Effie's baby came, she would love it best of all! A tremor of joy shook her, ending in a happy kick of her feet.

"What's a granny woman?" she wondered.

Swiney put down the kitten and picked up another. Its eyes were closed tight, and it cried a pitiful little mew as its tiny paws reached for its mother.

"It's an old woman that comes to birth the babies. She brings 'em with her, in a poke. Abe says there's a time you know when the baby's a-going to come, and then you send for the granny woman and she brings it."

Rose had seen creatures being born before. She had seen the hens laying their eggs, had watched Blackfoot's bedraggled kittens come one after another, and she had been in Alva's barn when one of their cows had a calf in her stall. Rose had cried at first when it fell to the floor and lay there perfectly still, not even breathing. Then the cow began to lick it and lick it. After a minute, the poor spindly calf raised its wobbly head, and before long it was standing on trembling legs sucking hungrily from its mother's bag.

But Rose had never seen a human baby being born, and she couldn't imagine anything so untidy as that. She certainly didn't want to think of herself having been born that way. Maybe a granny woman did bring them. But why was Effie getting fat? Rose wanted to ask Mama, but it was impolite to talk much about babies before they were born, and she was too shy.

After the garden was finished and the fences mended, they cleaned the house from top to bottom, airing the quilts and straw tick mattresses in between the rainstorms, washing and ironing the curtains, and scrubbing the whole floor with sand and lye soap.

The sun hardly showed itself for weeks. Papa, Abe, and Swiney stayed working in the timber lot. In between their regular chores, they went to Abe's little house and rolled logs to stack and dry for Abe's barn. They would build it in the fall, when the logs had cured properly.

Each wet morning after sunrise, Papa stood on the porch, pushed his hat up, and gazed at the low blanket of clouds and the steady drizzle, twisting an end of his mustache thoughtfully.

"Going to get a late start with plowing this year," he said one day. "It'll take a good week for the ground to dry and break proper, even if the rain would quit today."

"There's no loss without some gain," Mama said. "The soil is getting a good deep soaking. Once the crops are in, and the weather clears, they ought to come up fast."

But the rain didn't quit that day, or the next day either. It rained every day, coming hard and fast as bullets sometimes, then slowing to a fine mist that drifted down and touched the skin on Rose's arms, as soft and silky as morning glory petals. The air smelled fresh and clean, full of the odor of rotting leaves.

Mild breezes rustled through the bare trees, whispering of the return of life. In mud puddles Rose found tiny pollywogs the size of persimmon seeds wriggling joyfully. Pink buds began to swell on the apple trees, and mourning doves cooed wistfully from the meadows. Rose couldn't wait for spring to bring more color back into the world, and fresh greens to eat.

With winter's end came the end of school. On Monday of the last week, Blanche greeted Rose at the door of the Fourth Reader with a flushed face and a big grin.

"I'm having a birthday party on Saturday," she gushed, her black curls quivering with excitement. "You will come, Rose. Won't you?"

"Yes!" Rose cried out. "I must ask Mama, but I'm sure I will."

All that day, Rose thought about Blanche's party and wondered and worried. She'd never been to a party before. Her best dress was getting short and Mama had already let the hem out as much as she could. She said it would need a patch in the hem before long, too. Rose didn't want to just wear her school dress that Blanche saw every day. What could she do? And what could she take for a present?

"A kitten?" Mama said. "I don't know that a kitten is such a good present. Maybe the

Codays don't need a cat, and it would be giving them another mouth to feed. I have a nice piece of white linen in my scrap bag. Why don't you embroider it? Then we can finish the edges to make a handkerchief."

So Rose spent her spare time at night at the table in the soft yellow circle of lamplight, carefully stitching a design. She decided to sew a tiny pink rose blossom with two green leaves on its stem, and Blanche's initials beneath in navy. Mama finished the edges and Rose ironed it into a crisp square. The embroidery showed in a corner.

"Your handwork is very good," Mama said when it was done. "Blanche will be proud to carry it, even to church." Rose beamed with pleasure. She wrapped the handkerchief neatly in some store paper and put it in a drawer in her new chest.

The day before the party, when Rose came home from school, Mama met her at the door with a sly smile on her face. "Run upstairs and change out of your school dress," she said. That was always the first thing Rose did when she came home from school. She never had to be told. She knew Mama had a trick up her sleeve, so she dashed up the stairs.

Hanging from the clothesline in the corner she found a beautiful dress of sprigged white dimity. Rose snatched it off the line and took it by the window to see better. The snowy cloth was printed all over with tiny leaves and flowers in navy blue. The wide lace collar was tatted in the pineapple design that Mama liked so well, with lace sewn on the linen cuffs, and Mama's tight, perfect stitching all over.

And it had fluffy, soft leg-o'-mutton sleeves!

Rose heard Mama's footsteps coming up the narrow stairs. "Oh, Mama! It's beautiful," she cried out. She felt the smooth cool fabric, and pressed it to her nose to breathe in the starched new smell of it.

Mama stood in the doorway, her arms crossed, her face radiant. In her hand she held a wide ribbon of the same navy blue as the sprigging in the dress.

"And a new hair ribbon!" Rose shouted. She flung her arms around Mama's waist and squeezed as hard as she could. That dress was too good to be true, Rose's first lawn. That made her feel very grown-up.

"It's early for lawn, but the hot weather will be here soon enough," Mama said, picking a bit of thread from the collar. "I gave it a nice deep hem. It should last a long time, if you mind not to play rough in it."

On the floor were a new pair of Brogans, too. Rose hated clunky old Brogans and wished she had a pair of coin patent-leather high-topped shoes with heels, like the ones some of the town girls wore to school and church. But at least the new Brogans weren't scuffed and cracked. The new dress was long. Maybe no one would notice.

Birthday Party

The next day after dinner Rose was so fidgety Mama had to scold her to be still as she brushed and plaited her brown hair into one wide braid. That was the way Mama always wore her own hair, except when she went to church, or visiting. Then she put it up in a tight bun.

Next Mama tied on the big navy-blue bow. Rose had never had such a beautiful ribbon. Always before she wore two small bows, one on each braid. She wished she could wear her hair like Mama's every day.

When Mama had given the bow one last pat,

Rose jumped up and ran to peer into the little mirror on the wall over the washstand. She could see only parts of herself at one time, but the lace collar and the bow with the light shimmering all through the satin made her feel like a flower. She turned and smiled bashfully at Mama.

"You look just lovely," said Mama. "Now hurry and get going. It's too wet and muddy to walk. I sank to my ankles in the puddle just before the bridge. Papa will drive you to the party."

Papa carried Rose to the wagon and chirruped to the horses, and they headed down the slippery slope toward Fry Creek, and then up the hill to town. He had to stop now and then to clean great clumps of mud off the wheels and from the hooves of the Morgans.

Rose stayed huddled on the wagon seat holding her coat around her shoulders against the rain. The air was cool and damp, but she was too jittery to be cold. The breeze refreshed her, flowing over her cheeks like water.

Mama had pulled her bonnet on loosely over

the bow. Rose kept feeling the back of her head to make sure the bonnet wouldn't crush the bow. Her stomach churned a bit, and she kept checking to make sure she had remembered the handkerchief. It was safely tucked in a pocket of her dress.

They drove through the town square, which was bustling with wagons full of farm families come to town to do their trading. The relentless rain had turned the streets into rivers of mud, and all the horses were spattered with it. Then they turned away from the square onto a quiet side street lined with trees and beautiful houses all painted in dark colors.

When Papa *whoa*ed the horses in front of one of them and said, "Here we are!" Rose looked up and gasped. Blanche lived in the biggest house on that street. It was square and had two whole floors, and dormer windows peering out every direction from the roof. White smoke puffed from two of the three stone chimneys.

The house was painted a deep maroon, the color of plums, with dark brown shutters, and fine lace curtains in every window. Wicker rocking chairs sat on the porch, waiting for a warm sunny afternoon when someone would come sit in them and sip drinks of lemonade.

A brilliant green carpet of grass covered the yard, and on one side there was a mulberry tree, its branches blushing with heavy buds. And all around ran a fancy black-iron fence, with a gate in the middle of the front. Everything about that house looked tidy and lovingly cared for.

Papa climbed off the seat and lifted Rose down, setting her on the gravel sidewalk. His hat was soaked with rain, and his shoes were clumped with mud. Pet shook herself and whickered. A pair of jaybirds flitted past, loudly scolding. Rose untied her bonnet and handed it to Papa for safekeeping.

"I'll be back in a couple of hours to pick you up, before supper," Papa said, fixing her collar. He looked her all over and smiled. "You sure look sweet, my little prairie Rose. You're getting to be a big grown-up young girl. Won't be long before some young fella will be driving

you around. Then you won't need your old papa anymore."

"Oh, Papa, you're teasing." Rose giggled. She pecked him on his wet cheek. Then she let herself through the gate into the Codays' yard and walked up the gravel path straight to the porch.

Rose's stomach fluttered as she climbed the wide steps. She could almost have turned and run back to the wagon, she was so nervous. But she was drawn to the muffled sound of children's voices shouting and laughing that she could hear coming from inside.

She patted her beautiful bow. Before she could reach up and knock, the door flew open and Blanche was smiling at her from inside the house.

"I was worried you mightn't come," Blanche gushed. "It's just awful, all this rain we've been having. I so wanted for everyone to play croquet."

Inside the house was warm and cozy, and it smelled of fresh baked goods. Two boys came bursting out of the parlor through a bead portiere into the foyer, one chasing the other into a room to the side where all the children were playing. A great staircase with a rich brown railing and pearly white spindles rose up to the second floor.

Rose couldn't stop looking all around her at the lush flowered carpet and the little round table with a globe lamp sitting on a doily, and a red-and-blue china vase on the floor with a bouquet of umbrellas sticking out. She had never imagined anyone living in such a beautiful house.

Mrs. Coday's voice rose above the shrieks of little girls in the sitting room, and boys shouting. "You youngsters had better stay out of my parlor or I'll skin you alive!" she called out. Then she appeared in the doorway, carrying a tray of cookies. "Well, look who's here!" she cried out cheerfully. "Mansfield's number-one speller."

Rose felt her face grow warm as Mrs. Coday smiled at her. Everything was so clean and pretty and perfect in that house, Rose was afraid to take even a step. She stood with her back against the wall until Blanche took her hand and pulled her into the sitting room.

There were children everywhere in that room, some from school and a couple she did not know. Harry Carnall peered from behind a velvet settee, making a gun of his hand, shouting at Oscar Hensley, "I got you! I did! Dead men and ashes tell no tales."

"You didn't neither!" Oscar complained. He had a kerchief tied over his mouth and nose. "Hand over the payroll or I'll blow up your whole darn train."

"Oscar Hensley!" Mrs. Coday barked. "You'll mind your mouth in my house, or I'll be having a word with your mother. Now Blanche, why don't you show Rose the new stereographs?"

Blanche led Rose across the sitting room to the davenport, which was a beautiful cozy place to sit with a scalloped back that seemed to open up like a great clam, or a rosebud. A clutch of girls and two boys Rose had never met were gathered there. Cora and Dora Hibbard were there, and Blanche's cousin Lydia sat in the middle of them all, peering into something that looked like a pair of opera glasses, with a box attached to it.

"Let Rose have a look, Lydia," Blanche said. "She's just come."

"Say, I haven't seen this one yet," a dark-haired older boy complained.

"Never you mind, Scott Coday," Blanche scolded him. "This is my birthday party and no brother of mine is going to tell me who can look at my stereographs."

"This one is my favorite," Lydia said, shaking her buttery curls as she handed the stereoscope to Rose. A gold bracelet with a heart-shaped locket sparkled on her wrist. "It's the White City, at the World Exposition in Chicago. Well, it burned down, but we have a stereograph of the fire, too.

"Seeing it does make me miss Chicago so. I don't like to live in such a bitty little town." She wrinkled her nose so the freckles bunched together into a smudge. "There's nothing at all to do here."

"Yes there is," said Dora quickly. "There's the Opera House."

"Oh, that," Lydia said with a wave of her hand. "That's no better than an old cow barn. Chicago has dozens of opera houses, with big crystal chandeliers and tall curtains on the stage. We even have kinetoscope parlors, too. Just everywhere."

"What's that?" Dora wanted to know.

"It's a place to show actualities. Living pictures," Lydia said, picking up a cookie with her little white fingers, her pinkie sticking out. She nibbled a tiny bite. "Don't you know anything?"

Dora bit her lip and then went to get a glass of lemonade from Mrs. Coday.

Blanche showed Rose how to look into the stereoscope. The box had a handle to hold it up to your eyes. In the box there was a card, like a postcard only with two pictures exactly the same, side by side. That was a stereograph. The stereograph slid in and out, so you could look at different pictures.

The stereograph in the stereoscope was a picture of great buildings, as piled up and white as whipped cream. The buildings had pillars and domes and fluttering flags, and people standing in front of them. There was a canal running past those buildings. A long narrow boat with pointed ends floated in the canal, and a man wearing a striped shirt and flat black hat stood in the boat, holding a long pole.

But when Blanche held the stereoscope up to Rose's eyes, something wonderful happened to those pictures. They became one picture, and the boat with the man in it came right off the paper! It was as if he and the boat were really floating, as if you could see behind him, and behind the building, too! Rose felt herself being drawn into that picture, almost as if she were actually there in Chicago at the White City.

"Oh, Blanche!" Rose gushed. "It's magic!"

"Yes, Chicago is really very beautiful," Lydia said, patting down the lap of her red serge dress with a little tinkle of her bracelet. "Much nicer than here."

Rose bristled a little at Lydia's haughtiness, but she kept her thoughts to herself.

They all took turns looking at the other stereographs. There were so many, and each one was more exciting than the last. There were pictures of Indians and Indian fighters, of great machines with giant jaws carving out a canal across the Isthmus of Panama, of faraway island natives in dresses made of grass and hats made of wood and leaves and feathers.

On the back of each stereograph there was a caption explaining the picture. It was written six times, in six different languages, so all the immigrants who had come to America could read it too. Rose stared and stared at those foreign words that told her nothing, but others could read and understand as plain as English. She had never known there were so many languages in the world. She wondered what those languages sounded like when a person could speak them.

She tried to pronounce some of the words, but they just came out as senseless gibberish. A few of them were written with the same letters as English. Rose thought the words on the backs of those stereographs were just as interesting as the pictures themselves. She wanted to speak those languages and to understand them. There was a mystery locked in those strange-looking words, and she wanted to learn it.

"Well, I just don't know how you can bear it here," Lydia was saying to the Hibbard twins. "It's so poor-folksy, with all those farmers and raggedy children who come to town smelling so bad. Why, half the people here don't even wear shoes. And there isn't a thing in these stores I would ever want to wear."

"Oh, Lydia. Land sakes," Mrs. Coday said, tidying up the cookie tray and lemonade glasses on the table. "There you go again, finding the worst in everything. Chicago isn't the only place on earth, you know."

But Lydia just rolled her eyes and smirked.

Rose was growing impatient with Lydia. She looked at the beautiful bisque doll that Blanche's mama and papa had given her for her birthday.

"I'm getting too grown-up for dolls," said Blanche. "But I just love her, don't you? Here, you may hold her. You must help me think of a name."

Rose cradled the doll very carefully in her

arms. She was something to hold, very big, as big as a real baby, with big, surprised eyes, pink cheeks, and a tiny heart-shaped mouth painted bright as a cherry. Her pink dress was sewn of the sleekest silk.

She wore a cunning little jacket with puffed sleeves and embroidered cuffs. Her shiny brown hair was curled in long ringlets, and she had a matching hat trimmed with bows and lace. Her tiny shoes had real buckles, and she even had on stockings! Rose would give anything to have a dress as beautiful as that doll's.

The doll's arms and legs were jointed. Rose moved them so she was reaching out for a hug. Then Rose hugged her, very gently, so as not to crush her hat.

"And we have horseless carriages in Chicago, too," Lydia was saying. "Why, I shouldn't think you could ever have one here. The roads are so muddy and rutted. In Chicago the streets and sidewalks are paved as smooth as glass and a lady can go visiting without ruining her shoes or soiling her hem."

Rose laid Blanche's doll down on the little

round table that sat in the middle of the sitting room. She caught a glimpse of her clumsy Brogans. Hard as she had tried to keep them clean, there were splashes of dried mud around the edges of the soles.

She looked at Lydia's shimmering curls and her lovely dress, then at Blanche, who was wearing a delicately checked pink dress with a clever jacket that Blanche said was a bolero. Her cuffs were ruffled, and trimmed with fancy white braid. There was braid on her collar too, and her dress even had a braided belt. Her shiny patent leather shoes were pointed and dainty, and laced up the ankle.

Before she could stop herself, Rose's chest heaved with a sigh of envy. Then a wave of shame flamed up her neck.

Rose thought of Papa driving her to town when he should have been doing chores, spattered with mud and wet from rain, his work-battered hands still red from the raw winter cold. She thought of the pineapple lace collar that Mama had so carefully tatted, staying up late after Rose had gone to bed, working in the dim circle of lamplight at the kitchen table.

Two feelings fought inside her. She wished she could dress as finely as Blanche and Lydia, and curl her hair, and live with Mama and Papa in a house as fine as the Codays'. But then she swelled with fierce pride when she thought about how hard she and Mama and Papa were working to build up the farm. She thought about Abe and Swiney, too, and how hard they all struggled to survive in a new land, and still make time for small pleasures. It is the small things in life that matter, Mama had said.

Lydia's peevish voice interrupted Rose's thoughts again: "I should think anyone would rather live in Chicago than in such as boresome place as this. After all, anything a body could ever think to want or do is right—"

Rose stamped her foot in fury. A loud thump echoed in the room. Lydia stopped in the middle of her sentence and stared at Rose in wonderment. All the children's heads snapped around as they looked at Rose. Rose stared back at Lydia. Her mind was spinning and she didn't know what words might come out of her mouth. Then she blurted, "If you hate it here so, why don't you just go back to Chicago?"

Lydia's mouth dropped open, and her brows flew up. She stood and jammed her fists into her hips. Her eyes narrowed and glared down at Rose with hawkish fury. Her mouth wobbled and then pinched.

"I just will, Rose Wilder," she spat out. "Just as soon as Father sends for me. And I say good riddance to you and your sort when he does."

Rose's cheeks flamed hot. Her hands trembled. She wanted to slap Lydia, she was so mad. She could scarcely catch her breath. For an instant her mind went black with fury. Then it cleared, and she knew what she would say. She stood and took a big gulp of air.

"You are the most boastful, uppish thing I ever saw," she declared. "You don't care for anything but your own self."

Rose heard a gasp from behind her, where Mrs. Coday stood. But she couldn't stop herself now.

"Just how do you think you could eat if

farmers didn't grow your potatoes and onions, and send you milk and butter? How would you live in your wonderful Chicago then? You'd come begging to us for something to eat. And if you did, I'd give the crumbs from our table to my dog before I'd give any to you. If everyone in Chicago is like you, I wouldn't ever like to see it."

Lydia's eyes and mouth made big "O"s in her face. A red flag of rage flew upon each cheek. She looked at Blanche, who was still sitting on the davenport. She had a hand over her mouth and she was looking at Rose as if she had just seen a ghost.

"Blanche!" Lydia finally wailed. "Say something! How dare she speak to me like that! Make her go. This is your house, and it's your party. You can if you want to."

Blanche sat in stricken silence, looking from Rose to Lydia. Her mouth moved, but no words would come out.

"Well, say *something*!" Lydia demanded.

Seeing the look of horror on Blanche's face, Rose suddenly hated her own shameful behavior. It was wicked to speak to anyone unkindly.

"I'm sorry, Blanche," she said quickly. "I will go. I couldn't bear to stay."

Rose marched out of the sitting room into the foyer, her eyes stinging. She didn't dare turn around. She could feel all the faces staring at her from the sitting room as she stormed out the door.

But as she was pulling the door closed behind her, someone was tugging it open. Then Blanche was on the porch beside her. Her face was flushed, and Rose was shocked to see her mouth quivering in mirth.

Then Blanche burst out giggling. Rose stood there, dumbfounded.

"Oh, Rose. That was so *mean*," Blanche said, her giggling turning to laughter. "But she had it coming. How many times I wanted to say those very same things. But I never could. I'm so glad you did."

Rose felt her face relax; then she couldn't help giggling a little herself.

"I'm sorry," she said, feeling suddenly sober again. "It was wrong of me to spoil your birthday party."

"Oh, no!" Blanche exclaimed, hugging herself against the chill. "Don't be sorry. I'm glad, honest. I am so tired of her complaining. I wish she'd go back to her old Chicago." Blanche made a face and ground her fists into her hips the way Lydia had. Then they both burst out with hearty laughter.

Rose tucked her cold hands into her pockets.

"Oh!" she cried out. "I almost forgot. I made this for you." She pulled out the wrapped handkerchief and handed it to Blanche.

Blanche unfolded the delicate crinkly paper and looked at the handkerchief. She ran her finger over the embroidery. Rose waited breathlessly for her to speak. The soft rain made a gentle pattering sound as it dripped from the roof.

"It's the best gift I ever got!" Blanche finally breathed, looking at Rose with eyes that shone with pleasure and friendship. "You're the best friend anyone could ever have."

Rose blushed hard and stared at her shoes. "Thank you," she managed to mutter.

"Oh, Rose, won't you stay? I don't care what

Lydia thinks about anything. She ran crying to her room anyway. We can still have a pleasant time."

"Thank you," Rose said. "But it wouldn't be right, after I was so wicked."

"But didn't your Papa bring you?" Blanche insisted. "You can't walk home on the muddy roads. You ought to wait 'til he comes."

Rose wavered. She really did want to stay. She wanted to see more of Blanche's house, and to look at more stereographs. But she was too ashamed of herself to go back in and face the other children and Mrs. Coday. And she didn't want to see Lydia again for anything..

"I'll find Papa in town," she finally said. "He's doing errands, and I'll wait for him. Now you must come to my house one day."

"Oh, I will," Blanche said. Then she sighed. "Good-bye, Rose."

"Good-bye, Blanche," Rose answered. Then she walked down the path and let herself out the gate. As she turned to walk toward the town square she looked back. Blanche was still standing on the porch, waving. Rose waved back.

Growing Up

Rose walked slowly up the muddy street toward the square. She stayed on the gravel sidewalk, to keep any more mud from soiling her shoes. A soft, misty rain fell on the yards and chilled her. Her thoughts jumped around like grasshoppers. Rose would have to tell Mama that she had been rude to Lydia and had walked out of Blanche's party. Mama would be cross. A fresh wave of shame blazed through Rose.

Then she thought about Lydia, and about Chicago. She didn't like Lydia, but she would like to see Chicago. The stereograph of the

White City really was beautiful. And she would like to see the Isthmus of Panama, and the islands where people danced in grass skirts. Just imagining all those places and the people in those stereographs sent a jolt of excitement all through her.

Then a worry fluttered through her head: what if she couldn't find Papa? Rose had never been in town by herself. She wasn't sure where Papa was, or even where to look for him. But when she reached the corner of the the square and looked around, she spotted Pet and May hitched to the wagon in front of Young's livery stable. Her heart leaped for joy.

She walked down the sidewalk, past Mr. Coday's drugstore with its sparkling clean windows. Inside she could see shelves of brightly colored bottles and dazzling pictures on the walls.

Rose wanted to stop and look, but she saw Mr. Coday measuring out powders from a big jar onto a piece of paper. She hurried on, past the Opera House, Newton's Groceries, and the Boston Racket Store, with its windows filled with pots and pans and washtubs and bolts of fresh new fabric.

On the board sidewalks, her shoes made loud hollow noises that mixed with the rumbling of many other feet. The whole town was full of people bustling about on their errands. A few of them looked at her as they hurried by. A lady carrying an umbrella and wearing a big hat with feathers coming out all over smiled at Rose. That made her feel a bit odd, but she took a deep breath and held her head up. Then she felt very grown-up, walking in town all by herself on her very own errand. She was not the least bit scared. There was even something thrilling about being among strangers.

When she reached the livery stable, she hopped from one little solid island to another across the stable yard's sea of brown muck. She peered into the blackness beyond the wide yawning door. A man's voice laughed deeply. She could smell the rich scent of the horses, and hear them stirring restlessly in the stalls. But she could see only shadows.

Then she saw Papa standing next to a stall,

talking to Mr. Young. Some other men were sitting on chairs around the stable floor, whittling and spitting tobacco on the straw-covered floor.

Papa noticed her right away. He came striding over, stroking his mustache, a puzzled look on his face.

"Well, I'll be starched. You're a mite early. How'd you find me?" he asked. "Are you all right?"

"Yes, Papa," said Rose. "But I left the party early. Can we go home now?"

"Soon as I finish up with Mr. Young. You wait here. A livery stable's no place for a pretty young girl."

Rose waited patiently in the doorway until Papa finished. Then he untied the team, and they drove home. The wagon was spattered here and there with spring mud. The horses' brown backs and flanks were wet and dark and reddish mud speckled their bellies. They snorted irritably and tossed their heads as the wheels sucked noisily through the muddy tracks.

The wagon-box was piled with horse

manure. Wisps of steam curled into the cool damp air.

"Doesn't smell too good," Papa joked, jerking a thumb back over his shoulder. "But what you've got there is a pile of gold. And that smell's the smell of a cash crop."

"It is?"

"Yessir," said Papa. "That load of manure is food for the apple trees. And it's free. Young gives it away to anyone that wants it, just to get rid of it. We'll hoe it into the soil around the trees."

"How does horse manure feed apple trees?" Rose wondered.

"Can't exactly say as I know," said Papa, chirruping to the horses to pull through a deep, slippery puddle. The wagon lurched forward. Rose ducked as a clod of mud spurted from May's hooves and splashed against the dashboard. "I read about it in *Biggle's Orchard Book*. When the land's as thin and stony as ours, you've got to feed the orchard trees or they'll starve."

Rose wanted to tell Papa about the party,

and about the Codays' beautiful house and the stereographs, and about Lydia. But when she looked at Papa's weather-worn face, beaming with pride about their orchard, the words stuck in her throat.

So she listened quietly as he explained about feeding the soil, and plowing and hoeing to keep the moisture in, and pruning the trees so the middles would be open to sunlight, and the branches would be low enough to reach when they finally had a crop to pick. Papa loved to talk about the orchard.

Poor Fido was spattered with mud when he ran barking to meet them at Fry Creek. When they drove into the barnyard, Mama came out on the porch to greet them, wiping her hands on her apron. Rose's stomach clumped up like a clod of mud when she saw the questioning look on her face.

"You had no business speaking to her that way," Mama snapped when Rose told why she had left Blanche's party early. Mama shook her head as she strained the milk through a piece of cheesecloth. Her forehead knotted itself into a frown. "I taught you better than to let your mouth run away with you. Fetch me another milk pan."

"I couldn't stop myself, Mama. Lydia was so unpleasant. Even Blanche said—"

"Never you mind what Blanche said," Mama interrupted. "You showed disrespect to the Codays, too, and with no good cause, throwing common courtesy to the wind like that. I declare, Rose. You will learn a little patience or give yourself a name for having a sharp tongue. You will meet such people as Lydia the rest of your life."

She squeezed the last of the milk through the cloth with a hard twist. "The test of good manners is being respectful even to those with bad ones."

Rose sighed heavily and felt herself sag all over. She quietly tied on her apron and helped Mama cover the milk pans with clean cloths. Then they carried them carefully, so as not to spill so much as a drop, out to the porch where the cool air would bring the cream to the top.

When they were done, Mama sent Rose to

her room to change into her everyday dress. When Rose came down, Mama had made a pot of tea and was pouring two cups. They sat at the kitchen table, waiting for the tea to cool a bit.

"Well then," Mama said, her forehead smooth again. "Let's hear about the rest of the party, before you lost your head."

Rose told about the stereographs, and Blanche's doll, and the Codays' beautiful house with its plush carpets and glowing globe lamps and lace curtains. Mama listened quietly, murmuring her delight now and then.

"And after that, I got mad and went to look for Papa," Rose finished.

"Now, what was it that Lydia said that got your goat?"

"She said the people here are dirty and common and boresome, and everything is better in Chicago." Rose rambled on and on, telling Mama every word that Lydia had spoken. She was surprised to see a crinkle of humor around Mama's eyes and then a crooked smile on her lips.

"What is it, Mama? What are you thinking?"

"I was just remembering a little girl I knew, when I was a child," she said, pouring a bit of molasses into her tea. "She was unpleasant to me at my first party, too. Her name was Nellie Oleson, and she was a boastful, selfish little girl from back East. Her folks were rich then, as rich as one can be on the prairie. She had a mean streak a mile wide. Oh, I didn't like her the least bit."

Mama made a face, then she smiled again. "I tried never to show her my true feelings. I am sure that she was more unhappy than she could ever have made me. But one day she made me mad enough to want to repay her."

"What did you do?" Rose nearly shouted. She couldn't imagine Mama doing anything unkind to anyone.

Mama cuddled her cup in both hands and took a sip. The steam curled through her fringe bangs like fog in the trees. "I oughtn't to say. It wasn't very nice at all."

"Please!" Rose begged.

"Mmmm. Well, I suppose there's no real

harm in it," said Mama. Then she wagged a finger at Rose. "This is no example for you. I oughtn't to have done it, but I was little. You are a big grown-up girl now."

The story was about the time Mama tricked Nellie Oleson into wading a creek where Mama knew there lived a mean old crab, and blood-sucking leeches. Nellie had been disrespectful to Grandma Ingalls, and that made Mama hopping mad.

The crab chased Nellie into the dark water where the leeches hid, just the way Mama had planned. Rose laughed as hard as she ever had when Mama told how Nellie screamed and kicked when she came out from the water and found leeches stuck on her legs and feet. Even Mama had to laugh at the memory of it.

"And do you know, I had my justice twice, though the second time it was not my own doing, and it was many years later," Mama said, getting up to fetch a match. She lifted the lamp chimney and lit the wick. The flame fluttered to life, and its reflection danced in Mama's mirthful blue eyes.

"Nellie liked your father, and I believe she meant for him to ask for her hand. But of course he married me instead. You see, revenge is a dish best served cold. Remember that."

Rose guffawed. How could Papa ever have married anyone but Mama? If he had, there would be no Rose, and that was impossible!

Then she laughed a second time. Mama had named one of the stubborn, ugly mules Nellie. Now Rose knew why.

She loved the way Mama would tell a story on herself, about something foolish or amusing or interesting she had once done or seen. Those were moments when Rose knew how much she loved Mama, and how much Mama loved her back. It was a best-friend kind of feeling, different from everyday love.

"Tell me again about the time before you and Papa were married, when he came to fetch you in the blizzard," Rose begged. She could never hear enough of Mama's stories.

But Mama said it was time to get supper, and for Rose to bring in wood for the stove, feed and water the stock, and do all her other evening chores. "Another day," she promised.

As Rose carried armloads of hay to Bunting and Spark in the dairy barn, she carelessly splashed through the mud puddles in her cozy old shoes. Her heart felt light, and her head was clear.

Mama could be quick to scold, and she worried about things, Rose thought. She even got cross with Papa sometimes when he spent money for things they didn't really need, like the new cookstove or fancy brass fittings for the harness.

They couldn't live in a house as fine as the Codays had, or pay for a stereoscope. They would have to wait more years for the orchard to bear before they could have even a few things just for pleasure. But they had each other, and Rocky Ridge Farm with all its creatures to be protected and cared for, and the precious orchard to be nurtured.

Rose stroked the velvety hair on Spark's neck as he nuzzled a mouthful of hay. Bunting looked over her railing with curious eyes and lowed softly.

Talking with Mama had made Rose feel grown-up all over again. Every day she really was getting older, faster and faster, it seemed. Papa called her a young girl now, and she drank tea with Mama like a grown-up.

Rose realized with a shock that she didn't think like a little girl any longer, either. She wasn't afraid in town by herself, she hardly ever played with her rag doll anymore, and she often daydreamed about the hurrying trains and the whole unknowable world that lay beyond the mountains.

Right then and there, listening to the crunching sounds of the cows eating their supper, Rose made a promise to herself to fight her temper the next time someone's bad manners stirred her up. She would try to bide her time, the way Mama did. Rose didn't know if she could, but she would try with all her might.

Birthing Season

One day a great windstorm scoured the Ozark Mountains, thrashing the trees, rattling the windows and door, and howling down the chimney. It was so gusty that even Papa had to lean against the wind so he could walk between the house and the barns. The wind pushed Rose so hard that she had to run to keep from falling. It whipped her braids, and they flew about, lashing her cheeks.

When the first chickens came fluttering out for their breakfasts, the wind knocked them right down and sent them tumbling across the yard like tufts of milkweed, squawking loud complaints. Rose and Mama had to scurry to catch the hens and carry them back to the hen-house. After that the chickens stayed in all day.

Then the wind chased away the rain clouds and scrubbed the whole sky clean. That night, when Rose went outside to use the convenience, a bright carpet of stars lay over the earth and the mild night air was perfectly still. The song of the peeper frogs came loud and clear from the swampy place by Fry Creek.

In the morning, the sun quickly burned off the misty haze and rose bright and clear. It smiled tenderly on the hills and poured down its shimmering warmth on the sodden earth. The sky was so brilliant that it made the house and barns seem small.

The muddy soil began to dry, and the roaring voice of the water in the spring branch softened to a whisper. Here and there around the yards the first tender shoots of dandelion, lamb's-quarter, dock, and wild mustard poked shyly into the light. The air swam with the perfume of washed flowers and the rich, dark scent of freshly turned earth.

Rose stopped in the barnyard with an armload of stove wood, turned her face to the sun, and closed her eyes. The strong light made odd colorful patterns on her eyelids. A gentle warm breeze flowed over her bare arms and cheeks like caressing fingers. A pair of mourning doves called to each other in the timber lot: "*Coooo, coo-coo-coo.*" From all around her the forest birds warbled their high-spirited songs.

It was a wonderful, tingly feeling, to know that the long, gray waiting time of winter was truly over, and life was beginning again. Rose felt as if she had lived for the longest time like a mouse in a hole. Now all of her overflowed with energy, and she dashed across the yard to the house. Just as Fry Creek had pressed against its banks after the spring rains, life swelled in her veins.

Every sight and sound struck her senses with freshness. There was newness even in the bite of cold water on her skin when she washed up for breakfast in the tin basin on the bench by the door. Mama whistled as she cooked. The smell of coffee and frying salt pork was especially good, and Rose sang along as she spread the red cloth on the table and set out the plates: *"Oh, Susanna, Oh, don't you cry for me. I've come from Alabama with my banjo on my knee."*

Almost in a single day, it seemed, the whole earth blushed. On the hillsides, the barren trees turned a misty pink. The buds on the redbud and apple trees swelled. Papa hurried everyone out to the orchard to thin the apple buds before they opened. Rose hated picking off the tender bulging nubs that were just about to burst open into beautiful white flowers, but Papa said that *Biggle's Orchard Book* told him to do it. "Saves the strength of the young trees for making more wood," he explained. "An apple tree needs to grow strong limbs, to hold up the fruit."

The sun shone every day now, and the earth turned solid underfoot for the first time in weeks and weeks. Mama sent Swiney and Rose out to follow Bunting and Spark into the pasture, to gather greens. That way they could know which ones were safe to eat. Whatever the cows ate, they could eat too. Rose especially loved the wild onions, and she ate every one she found. After the long winter, fresh greens were as good as sweets again—even better.

The garden began to sprout the first shoots of carrots and radishes. In no time at all they had lettuce leaves big enough to pick. Mama served them up in vinegar and sugar.

It was birthing season. All around them, the creatures of the world had their babies. One night after supper Pet, one of Papa's Morgan mares, foaled. Rose watched the colt come into his new world, and fetched a pail of warm water from the cookstove and a clean dry cloth so Papa could help Pet clean him up.

Papa was very gentle with the colt. All the while he was washing and drying him, he talked softly to Pet, who paced and watched him fretfully. "That-a-girl, Pet. You're a good mother," Papa crooned. Then Pet understood, and she began carefully to lick the helpless little colt's long, slender neck and forehead.

In no time at all he was all dried and standing

on trembly fine legs, nursing greedily. The colt's soft, bright-brown hair shone like velvet in the lantern light. He had a small white star in the middle of his forehead, just like Pet and May had. Papa stood back, put his hands on his hips, and beamed with pride.

"Nothing beats a Morgan for good breeding," he crowed. "That little shaver has perfect lines and not a blemish on him. He'll be fast on a buggy, too."

Rose's heart filled with an unspeakable joy. She loved all creatures on a farm, but none so well as a colt. The dark, liquid eyes looked curiously at everything, the ears fluttered this way and that like birds, and she thought nothing was more beautiful and fascinating than to see colts racing across a pasture, kicking up their dainty heels.

She spent every spare minute after that in the barn watching the colt explore the stall on his slender legs, nuzzling Pet's belly, or just lying in the straw resting. She wanted more than anything to stroke his long delicate neck and scratch his forehead under the wispy forelocks. She pined for the day when she could currycomb him, and brush and braid his black mane and long black tail.

But Papa was very strict about the colt. When Swiney came to see the colt, he stuck his hand through the rails to touch him when he wandered near the stall gate. The colt snorted and shied. Papa came quickly striding from the other end of the barn, where he had been pitching hay into May's stall.

Without a word, he took Swiney's arm and firmly pulled him away from the gate. "You youngsters must keep away from him," Papa solemnly said. One at a time, he looked Rose and Swiney straight in the eyes. He almost never used his sober voice, or looked at them so hard. Rose and Swiney listened quietly.

"If I learned one thing from my father it was that in five minutes you can teach a colt tricks it would take months to gentle out of him. They're high spirited and easily ruined. Mind what I tell you, a colt as fine as that can be worth more than this whole farm."

Papa knew everything about Morgans and

about Morgan colts. Rose's grandpa Wilder had raised Morgans, and Papa had helped care for them as a boy. Papa said that Morgans were the best horse a farmer could have: "Pound for pound, the most beautiful, strongest and best-tempered beast to walk this earth." All Papa's life, he would have no horse but a pure Morgan.

After some days, Papa declared that he would name the colt Royal, after Papa's older brother. "He was the crown prince of our family, when I was a boy," he said. "And this foal is ours."

It was a good name for the colt, Rose thought. He was handsome and fine as a royal prince.

Now the hens began to hatch out their spring broods. Mama put them up in coops in the barn, where Fido could watch over them and keep them safe from hawks and snakes.

In the early mornings just before sunrise, when flags of mist drifted above Fry Creek, Rose sometimes caught sight of a mother rabbit with four little ones, nibbling on a patch of clover that grew near the garden.

She and Swiney hunted quail nests along the pasture fences and found the scattered bits of their eggs after the babies had hatched.

Even the insects had their babies. Mud daubers crawled out of their clever tunnels on the barn walls, and hurried right to work, buzzing along the eaves of the barn and house hunting spiders.

Effie's baby still han't come. She stayed home now. Mama said Effie was busy with her own spring cleaning chores. One day, when Rose went visiting with Alva, they found Effie sitting down in her kitchen, dabbing with a handkerchief at her forehead and neck. Rose was surprised to see Swiney standing at the stove, stirring a pot of beans.

Swiney blushed hard to be caught doing kitchen chores, but Rose thought it was wonderful how gentle and kind he had become. Effie had been a taming influence.

Effie smiled weakly. "I'd get up and fetch you young'uns a drink of water but I'm a-feeling puny and wore out." She patted her bulging stomach. "I've got so big I cain't hardly stand on my own two feet."

It was true. Effie looked as if a watermelon

were growing inside her dress. Rose blushed just to see it. She realized with a shock that there really must be a baby in there. Where else could it be?

Then she wondered how a baby could possibly breathe inside its mother. How could it get its food? Royal had lived inside Pet before he was born. All those kittens had lived inside Blackfoot, and the baby chicks had lived inside their shells before they pecked their way out.

She walked home with Alva along Fry Creek. All around them the earth was giving birth, and Rose's head swam with questions she dared not ask.

Boom Town

The weeks of spring flew by, and the air turned steadily warmer. The earth bloomed like a green cloud, and every morning Papa brought Mama a new bouquet of flowers for the kitchen table.

The days were full of hoeing and weeding the garden and planting corn and spring house-cleaning. The weather stayed pleasant, with thunderstorms coming every few days, but not so much rain as to hurt the plants.

The corn sprouted fast and began to unfurl its bright-green leaves to flutter in the breezes like tiny flags. Papa said the corn was late, but the wet spring had soaked the ground and given it such a strong start that it would catch up.

Then one morning right after the corn had sprouted, Papa came rushing into the house after breakfast. He grabbed his rifle from the rack by the door. "Durn crows in the corn patch!" he growled as he flew out the door. Running after him, Rose caught sight of a whole flock of crows in one corner of the field, tugging with their beaks at the precious sprouts.

The greedy crows fought with each other over the tenderest shoots, flapping their wings and calling out in their hoarse voices. Papa raised his rifle to fire, but the crows quickly flew away, disappearing into the trees at the far end of the field. From their hidden perches they cawed in mocking voices.

Papa went out to the cornfield with his rifle each morning for a week, hoping to catch the crows stealing the sprouts. But the crows were too smart. They always had a scout sitting high up in a tall tree. As soon as Papa came near the cornfield, the scout crow called out loud and fast, "*Caw-caw-caw-caw-caw*." Instantly all the crows in the field sprang into the air and flew away.

Papa couldn't stay in the cornfield all day, so he took Fido and tied him to a fence post. Poor Fido didn't understand, and he whined piteously when Papa walked away. It broke Rose's heart to see him tied up, but someone must guard the corn. It was the food they must have to get through the next winter, to feed the stock and themselves.

Even with Fido tied up in the field, after a week the crows had eaten up nearly half the shoots. Then they grew tired and flew away to pester something else. Papa, Rose, and Mama had to replant all that corn. Now half the corn would be late, for sure.

Next Papa and Abe cut the first crop of hay. They left it on the ground to cure for a day or two. But the next morning after cutting, a sudden rainstorm blew up, and all the hay got wet. It was ruined, and Papa had to leave it on the ground to rot.

But even with the crows, and the ground-hogs and other creatures that came at night to nibble the garden plants, and the late corn, and the lost cutting of hay, Papa said it was sure to be a good year. "The best we've had yet in Missouri," he promised. "Things always turn right side up in the end."

In the evenings after supper, Rose and Mama sat on the breezy porch, knitting and sewing for Effie's baby. The air was sweet with the smell of dewy clover. The birds twittered sleepily, and the tree frogs and katydids rehearsed their night chorus. Mama's chair creaked as she rocked and sewed.

The last of Blackfoot's kittens sat at Rose's feet, batting at a bit of thread that hung from Rose's dress. Papa had given away all of the other kittens in town.

Effie was praying for a boy, so Mama had sewn up a dainty pink gingham dress with a long skirt. Pink was the color for boys. Mama was knitting up two pairs of tiny woolen socks, and Rose was finishing the last of four neatly notched stomach bands she had sewn out of white flannel. The bands would protect the baby's belly button until it healed.

"What if it's a girl?" asked Rose.

"I can always trim the dress up with blue ribbon," Mama said, biting off a piece of thread.

"When will the baby come?" Rose wondered.

"Soon enough, I reckon," said Mama.

Rose bent to her stitching again, thinking. It took her some time to work up the courage, but finally she asked Mama the question that had been in her mind for the longest time.

"Mama, is the baby really inside of Effie? Is that where it comes from?"

Mama chuckled. "Of course it is," she said. "You can see with your own eyes how big she's become. Where else could it be?"

"Swiney said an old lady brings it, in a poke," said Rose.

Mama chuckled again, and scratched at a chigger bite on her ankle. From the valley came the sound of a rumbling wagon. Fido jumped up from his favorite lying spot by the oak tree and scampered off down the wagon tracks toward the creek. Papa was on his way home from town, where he had gone to get the plow repaired.

Across the barnyard near the redbud bush a

pair of greedy robins hopped about, hunting in the dead leaves for a last grub before bedtime. Long fingers of light from the setting sun pierced the trees and fell on the barnyard like splashes of melted butter.

"A person is born the same way a calf or a horse is born," Mama said. "Any story Swiney tells you is just some foolishness."

Then Rose took a deep breath and asked, "How does it get there?"

"How does what get where?"

"Who puts the baby there? How does it get inside its mother?"

The rocking chair stopped creaking and Mama's head jerked up. The needle froze in the middle of a stitch. She shot a sharp, questioning look at Rose. Rose flushed hot and looked down at her work. She was embarrassed, without knowing what she was embarrassed about.

Mama cleared her throat and stared into her lap. Her chair began rocking again, but there was agitation in its creaks. "I . . . you . . . Well, such a question, Rose!" she blurted. Rose looked at Mama in wonderment. Mama always had an

answer for everything. Now her eyelashes fluttered with uncertainty and she bit her lip.

Finally she sighed. "It is . . . it is one of life's
mysteries. A grown-up mystery that you will
know soon enough. When you are married,"
she quickly added.

When I'm married! Rose thought. I'm only
ten and a half years old! It would be years and
years before she would be married. Rose sighed.

The clomping sound of the horses' hooves
came from the bridge over Fry Creek, and
Fido's excited barking echoed up through the
trees. Mama jumped to her feet and set her
sewing down on her rocking chair.

"Well, then. Here is Papa at last. I hope he
remembered the mail. You'd best put up your
sewing and help him settle the mules for the
night."

Rose took the stomach band inside and
tucked it into a drawer in the little dresser in
her upstairs room. She was confused and, in a
way, more wondering than ever about babies,
and why Mama wouldn't tell her where they
came from. It seemed sometimes that the more

she understood things, the more questions she wanted to ask.

That Sunday the Cooleys came to dinner. They were all moved in to their new house in town, just over the hill, a short walk away.

Before dinner Rose showed Paul and George the bee gum in the orchard, and told them how Abe had taught her how to course a bee tree, and to rob the honey. George played Tug-of-War with Fido with a stick, while Rose and Paul watched the bees landing and taking off.

Paul said he was going to work with his father, driving the depot delivery wagon, and helping out in the freight office. Paul was getting so grown-up, Rose thought. He didn't look or act so much like a boy anymore.

Paul had always looked as sloppy as an unmade bed, with his shirt half pulled out, and his straw hat grimy and frayed. Now he kept his thick black hair combed neatly and wore a man's hat. When he spoke she noticed the little bump of his Adam's apple bobbing up and down, and his voice had a raspy sound to it.

"Someday I'm going to be a telegrapher," he declared importantly.

"What's a telegrapher do?" Rose asked.

"He sends telegraphs, of course. Papa's going to help me get a position, soon as I finish school. But first I have to learn the Morse code. That's a special language for sending telegraphs."

Then he took a stone and made tapping noises on a rock.

"That means, 'Clear track for express.' "

Rose was fascinated. She made Paul tell her all about the Morse code, and about the dots and dashes that stood for letters of the alphabet. He taught her how to tap out her own name: $\cdot - \cdot$, $- - -$, $\cdot \cdot \cdot$, $\cdot$ was R, O, S, E.

Rose looked at Paul with admiration. What a wonderful thing it was, to know another language and to sit in Mansfield and send messages far away to other people who knew the same language. It was too fantastic to imagine.

At dinner, Mr. and Mrs. Cooley talked excitedly about their house and their new life.

"I cherish the peace and quiet," Mrs. Cooley gushed, her eyes shining brightly. "Of course,

there are still the trains at our back door. I have
to remember to take the wash in before the
locomotives pass by, or my sheets will be soiled
with coal soot. And we're going to take in
boarders. Even so, the house is nicely laid out
for our own privacy."

Mr. Cooley worked at the depot now. He
wrote freight orders, weighed boxes and barrels, collected money for the railroad, and made
sure that there were enough cars in the depot
to load the crop harvests and timber and butter
and eggs—all the things the farmers sent to the
cities.

"Wilder, I can hardly believe it after the hard
times we've seen, but this town's on a boom,"
Mr. Cooley declared as he and Papa lit their
after-dinner cigars. "Mansfield's the fastest
growing town in Wright County, even faster
than the county seat at Hartville. And it's all on
account of the railroad. Some days I can hardly
find the cars for all the goods going out from
the depot. Some railroad men have been in
town, looking to lay a spur line down to Ava.
That'll mean even more commerce here.

"And there were some big-city fellas in town the other day, lawyers from a big mining outfit back East in Pennsylvania. Talking about starting up a lead and zinc mine just west of town.

"In a few years the whole town'll be strung for telephones. And some folks are trying to get some Wild West shows to come here: Buffalo Bill and Frank James, Jesse's brother. That'll bring folks from as far away as Arkansas. Think of the trade it'll bring!"

Rose and Paul and George all looked at one another with raised eyebrows. A Wild West show! With real-life Indian fighters, and bank robbers! Right in Mansfield! They couldn't wait.

"Yessir, this town's on a boom," Mr. Cooley said. "A lot of farmers don't like the railroads. The rates are high, and they don't care much for the little man. But without the trains, this town'd be nothing more than a bump on a turtle."

"Prosperity and progress are fine things," said Mama, scraping up a last bite of strawberry pie. "But there's no gain without some small loss. Every newspaper I pick up is full of train robberies and holdups."

"Tell 'em about the holdup at Macomb, Papa," George begged. "They blew up the train," he announced to everyone with a smug grin.

"Oh, George, really," Mrs. Cooley scolded. "Such a gruesome interest."

"Macomb!" exclaimed Papa, leaning forward. "Why that's just a few miles from here, the next depot east from Mansfield."

"It's quite a case," said Mr. Cooley, ignoring Mrs. Cooley's disapproving frown. "I'm surprised you didn't hear of it. But it just happened yesterday. Seems this young scalawag got on the train at Cabool and paid short fare to Springfield. When the train got to Macomb the conductor told him he had to pay the full fare or leave the train. Then the fella pulled a gun.

"Just then a second man climbed up into the smoking car and fired a couple of shots into the roof. And a third man climbed up on the engine and threw the engineer and express agent off the train.

"He told 'em if they valued their lives, they'd

better run down the track far as they could. Then the robbers dynamited the express car, grabbed the money out of the safe, and rode off on their horses."

"Land sakes!" said Mama. "I hope they catch them. I wouldn't want to think of desperados running loose in our fields."

Rose felt the hair on the back of her neck crawling. To think, train robbers might be hiding somewhere close by, maybe even in Williams Cave, across Fry Creek. Those men robbed the very train that passed by Rocky Ridge Farm every day!

"I shouldn't worry if I were you," Mr. Cooley said. "The conductor told me they got a good look at those robbers, and they rode off toward Norwood, to the east. I reckon those boys'll be behind bars by now."

Mr. Cooley knew many interesting stories about the railroads.

"Met a fellow the other day who told about an engineer down in Arkansas. He was barreling along when he looked down the track and spotted a bit of newspaper blowing about.

Didn't think much of it 'til it seemed to move sort of funny.

"He sharpened his look and saw it wasn't a bit of newspaper at all, but a baby in his diaper, toddling along, crawling right down the middle of the tracks."

Rose gasped, and Mama's hand flew to her mouth.

"That engineer threw the brake, but he could see plain as pudding it was no use. He had a heavy load of timber riding behind. The train could never stop in time.

"The poor man was beside himself to do something. So he crawled out of the cab, along the footboard by the side of the boiler, and then down right onto the pilot, at the very front. He could've fallen off and gotten killed himself."

Mr. Cooley stopped to strike a match and relight his cigar. Everyone sat still as hunting cats, ready to pounce on Mr. Cooley's next words. Rose took a deep breath.

"Well, the brakes were jammed hard and the wheels were grinding and screeching, and the train was going slower and slower. But it was going to catch that baby. The engineer sat himself down on the pilot, just above the rails, and when the train was right about to run over that child, he reached down with both arms and scooped it up."

"Oh my!" Mama cried out.

Rose let out a little scream. Then she giggled at herself.

"Even if it's a tall tale, that's a good one," Papa said, slapping his knee.

That night as she drifted toward sleep, the long, plaintive wail of a train whistle threaded its way through the warm night air. A limb of the oak tree outside her open window groaned in the wind, and the sound sent shivers up Rose's spine. A horse snorted. She sat bolt upright, her eyes straining to see in the darkness. She listened for a long time and decided it was just one of the mares, safe in its stall in the barn. She flopped back on her pillow, wide awake now.

She hoped those desperados were in jail, after all.

The Granny Woman

Rose slapped at a horsefly that had landed on her neck. But she was too late, it had already stung her. She tore off her bonnet. With a hand slippery with sweat and gritty with dirt she rubbed the painful bump that was rising on her neck. She threw down the hoe in disgust and went to sit in the shade and mutter complaints to herself.

It was only May, but summer was already building up in the Ozarks, like a kettle of water about to boil over on the stove. Rose would have given anything to go and soak herself in Fry Creek, or visit Blanche in town, or

go to the Bairds' and sit with Effie. But there
was always too much work to do.

Every year since they moved to Rocky
Ridge Farm Papa had plowed new ground.
Every year there were more crops to hoe, more
slimy cutworms to be plucked from the heads
of cabbages, more sprouts to be hacked from
the stumps of felled trees.

Rose sat for a long time, watching the quivering air rise in waves from the garden soil.
The heat had a heaviness that bore down on
her lungs like iron bands. She wished for a
breeze or a rain shower to cool things off. But
the weather had turned dry, and even the
thunderstorms that sometimes came at night
couldn't quench the heat. She tossed and
turned in her upstairs bed and the mornings
dawned hot and stifling.

Fido's tail and back feet poked out from
under the porch where he lay panting like a
lizard in the cool dirt. Blackfoot paced up and
down the porch twitching the end of her
upraised tail from side to side.

Mama came out on the kitchen porch and

threw a pan of dishwater on the little lilac bush Papa had planted by the steps. She wiped her brow with her apron and went back inside.

Papa was plowing the corn with the mules. He wore a wet cloth in the crown of his hat to keep his head cool, and he put old hats on the mules, too, with slits cut in them for their ears to poke through. A plume of gray dust followed them up and down the rows. Abe was by the barn, hammering out a bent point on his own plow.

The sun was a sore eye staring down at all the earth from the thin, high sky. It was too hot during the day even for the forest birds to sing, and the cicadas were muted. Only the mourning doves continued their sad cooing. Finally Rose sighed, got to her feet, and went back to hoeing the potatoes.

Rose was just about to go to the spring for a drink of cool water when she heard hooves clomping loudly on the bridge. A moment later Swiney came flying into the barnyard on the back of one of Abe's mules. The poor mule was soaked and lathery. Swiney had lost or forgotten his hat, and he had a scared look on his face.

He rode right up to the porch, jumped down, and ran inside, without even tethering the mule. Abe jumped up and followed him. Rose dashed to the house.

"It's Effie, Missus Wilder!" Swiney was crying out. "She's got her time. She's hollering something terrible. We got to get the granny woman quick!"

Abe's face had a helpless, frightened look Rose had never seen before. "Oh, Lord," he moaned. "Oh Lord, I hope there's time."

A tingle ran up Rose's legs. Mama hurriedly untied her apron. Her face was set, her mouth a thin line. But she did not look the least bit scared.

"Run and fetch Papa," she said briskly. "Run quick as you can."

Rose dashed out to the field, her heart in her mouth. Her breath came in painful sobs. She sprinted on bare feet across the hot dust to where Papa had stopped plowing to fix the harness. There wasn't a moment to spare.

"Papa, Mama says to come quick. It's Effie's time."

Papa unharnessed the mules and trotted them up to the barnyard. Swiney was leading May out of the barn. Abe was already back on his tired mule. Mama came out of the house with her bonnet on, carrying a sack of clean cloths, baby clothes, and the stomach bands.

"Manly, hurry over to the Stubbinses' and tell Mrs. Stubbins to send for the granny woman," she said. "Abe and I are going over to see about Effie. Rose, you and Swiney stay here and watch the place. Put the mules in the barn. We may be a long time. Remember all your chores."

Mama and Abe trotted off across the bridge. Then Papa was on May, galloping off to the Stubbinses'. Rose stood on the porch with Swiney in stunned silence until the barnyard was quiet again. The low mutter of distant thunder rolled toward them from the west. One of the chickens cackled loudly. Rose and Swiney sat down side by side on the porch steps.

Swiney shook his head slowly. His damp hair clung to his temples and his face was still flushed from the hard ride and the heat. "Golly, I never did hear anything like Effie's squalling. She told me to put the axe under the bed, to cut the pain, but she was hollering all the same. I hope that granny woman comes and brings that baby quick."

"Granny women don't bring babies," Rose said. "Mama told me." One of the hens squawked loudly again. The rooster was chasing it across the barnyard. Rose picked up a pebble and shied it at the rooster to make him stop.

"I know that," Swiney said. "I studied on it and figured it for myself. But Abe says a mama still needs a granny woman, to help her. A granny woman knows about yarbs and teas and such, to make the baby come easy."

Rose felt queasy and prickly from the heat and excitement. She had wanted to go with Mama and Abe, but she was glad not to hear Effie's cries. Rose hated to see any creature in pain.

That was a long hot wait. Rose went about her work with one ear cocked for the sound of a horse. How long did it take for a baby to come? she wondered.

She and Swiney hoed in the garden. Little

gusts of scorching air like invisible flames came up and licked their faces.

Without stopping the rhythm of her hoe, Rose glanced toward town. Three thin thunderheads lay low in the distance, peering over the edge of the hill. A few more clouds started to gather in the higher air. Rose hoped for rain. The garden could use some dampness, and it might cool the air some.

The gusts of wind stopped. The shimmering air seemed so light that Rose had to take a deep breath to fill the emptiness in her lungs.

Finally she heard a wagon rattling along Fry Creek. Fido barked and ran toward the creek.

"Someone's coming!" Rose shouted. "It must be the granny woman."

They dropped their hoes and ran down the wagon tracks. Papa rode up to the bridge. Mrs. Stubbins was behind him in a wagon, driving a team of mules. An old, old woman, her face as wrinkled as a dried apple, sat next to her on the seat.

"Any news?" Papa asked hurriedly.

"No, Papa," said Rose. "We were hoeing the garden."

"I'll be back in a flash. I've got to go in the house and fetch a few things your mama might need."

Then Papa chirruped to May and trotted up the hill.

Rose and Swiney stared at the old woman in the wagon. She wore a big, floppy black bonnet with wisps of gray hair sticking out the edges. Her dress was black, too. Her hands were as bony as the gnarled roots of a tree, her face as deeply creased as a weathered plank. She peered down at them with large, grave eyes. Blue fires glowed in their calm depths, brightening her pale face. Her puckered mouth worked her lips over her teeth.

"Are you going to bring Effie's baby?" Rose asked shyly.

The old woman nodded her head and her eyes blinked as slowly as a turtle's. Then she reached into her apron and pulled out a corncob smoking pipe. She lit a match and drew the flame into the pipe, and she blew out a big puff of smoke.

Rose was shocked. She had never seen a woman smoke before.

Swiney paced back and forth.

"You got to hurry along, or you'll be too late for her," he pleaded. "She's in a bad way. I saw her with my own eyes."

Mrs. Stubbins sighed fretfully. "I do hope she's all right. The first one's always the hardest. The poor thing."

The granny woman took another big puff from her pipe. She let her hand fall into her lap and looked down at Swiney.

"Child," she said, her great eyebrows working. "How old you be?" Her quavery rough voice made Rose think of pebbles. Her short, crooked teeth were stained yellow.

"I'm . . . I'm ten years old, I think," Swiney said.

The granny woman's face softened, and a cackle jerked from her throat. She leaned forward and fixed Swiney with an owlish stare.

"Granny Albers been a-ketching babies afore

your ma and pa was birthed," she said in her gravelly voice. "Just maybe I even ketched you when you come. Ain't hardly a soul 'round these yere mountains but I heared their first crying, and give 'em their first hug and bath, afore I even set 'em in the arms of their own mamas.

"Now in all them years I ain't missed a baby yet. Ketched ever' one I aimed to. Don't you be a-fretting yourself so. Ain't a body knows more 'bout a-ketching babies than Granny Albers."

Then she stuck the pipe in her mouth and folded her arms across her chest. Rose couldn't tear her eyes from Granny Albers. She wanted her to speak again, to hear her throaty voice, and to see the way her bushy gray brows arched and her eyes flashed. But the old woman just sat there in the hushed heat like a queen on her throne, patiently puffing her pipe and staring out at the creek and the forest beyond.

When Papa came back, there was a sack tied to his saddle with the extra washpan.

"I'm going to see these ladies over to Abe's place," said Papa. "But I'll be back in a wink."

A loud growl of thunder made them all look up at the western sky. One of the Stubbinses' mules slobbered and snorted in surprise, and the team backed the wagon up. Mrs. Stubbins had to scold them to be still.

Above Patterson's Hill, most of the sky was still burning blue. The lazy thunderheads were piles of gray with silver edges, but another clump of clouds to the north looked dark and angry. Lightning flickered and crackled along its black edge. A single gust of wind lifted Rose's skirt. There was a hint of coolness in it, the smell of hail.

"We best get a hustle on," Papa said, holding on to his hat. May pranced nervously. "Looks like we're in for a storm. You and Swiney hurry now and get the cows up from the pasture. You best get the chickens inside, too."

Then he rode off, the wagon rumbling behind him.

Rose and Swiney stood rooted to the ground, watching Papa and Mrs. Stubbins and Granny Albers go. But another wave of thunder woke them into action.

256

They dashed up the hill and past the barn to the cow pasture. They were in such a hurry that they knocked down a fence rail with a loud clattering. That startled Bunting, and she ran off with her tail high, Spark tagging along after her.

They had to chase Bunting around the pasture a long time to get her and Spark to walk back toward the barn. The claps of thunder were louder now, but the air was strangely, deathly still. Nothing stirred or spoke. The birds had ceased their chirping. The grasshoppers had stopped their fiddling. Only Fry Creek continued its foolish chuckling. The whole forest seemed to be hiding, listening and waiting for the storm to break.

A big gust of wind swirled through the barnyard as Rose and Swiney finally closed the heavy door of the dairy barn. The air filled with dust. The barnyard was still bright with light from the lowering sun, but the black angry cloud was nearly overhead.

They chased as many chickens as they could into the henhouse, but some of the chickens ran for the barn, and one darted under the kitchen porch. Fido was nowhere to be seen.

A wave of panic rippled through Rose's body. Sweat ran down her forehead and stung her eyes. There was something terrible coming in those clouds, she could just feel it. They must save Mama's hens.

Rose was by the smokehouse, trying to scoop up one of the pullets, when she heard Swiney's voice cry out, "Rose, look! Something big's burning!"

Swiney pointed to a tall black cloud in the shape of a trumpet, or the smoke from a locomotive. It soared far up into the sky, into the high clouds. The top end was bigger, and tapered down to a slender tongue at the bottom. But Rose noticed that the upper end was whirling and writhing. It was sucking smaller clouds into it.

Then she heard a sound like the roaring of a train, but there were no tracks where that cloud was. The light dimmed and went out, plunging the forest into a dusky gloom.

Rose's heart leaped into her throat. She opened her mouth to shout but the words wouldn't come. She gasped for breath.

A cyclone was coming!

Cyclone!

Rose's legs had turned to stone. She was senseless with fear and too bewitched to think of running. And even if she could have lifted a foot to run, she could not have thought where.

Nothing terrified her more than a cyclone. She had read stories in the newspapers: A cyclone could toss a whole house through the air and smash it to bits. A cyclone could crush a man in an instant.

The roar was growing louder, and quickly, too. The black cloud towered over everything. It boiled and churned and twisted like some hideous angry snake. Its long vicious tongue flicked at the earth.

The inky mass was streaked with livid green. It coiled in on itself and then thrust out. The flaring lightning flashed in hues of red and green. It roared like some awful beast from a nightmare.

Something struck Rose on the head, jarring her back to her senses. A hailstone, big as a quail egg, lay at her feet. Then all the roofs exploded with pounding. The ground erupted with a thousand dancing hailstones. A big gust of chilly wind slapped Rose hard in the face and she shivered.

"We've got to hide!" she screamed. Swiney stood stock-still, his mouth gaping open. Rose grabbed him by the straps of his overalls and pulled him toward the house. "Come on! Hurry!"

He stumbled after her, and finally began to run with her.

Just before they ducked inside, Rose turned on the porch for one last look. In those few seconds the funnel had covered the whole sky. It

stared cruelly down at her, ready to pounce and squash her like a small, helpless bug. Her whole body quaked uncontrollably. Tears welled in her eyes.

The edges of the funnel cloud had turned blurry. Then she saw something that made her feel sick to her stomach. In the blurry edge two cows were flying through the air!

Rose ran inside the house.

"In here! In here!" Swiney screamed above the deafening roar. Rose ran into Mama and Papa's bedroom. Swiney was scrambling under the bed. Rose dove after him. They scrunched themselves up as far under as they could. A great blast of air slammed against the walls. The little house shook and creaked and groaned with the howling wind. The floor shuddered beneath them. The weight of the wind pressed against their faces and arms. Then Rose's ears popped.

Now the air was shrieking, clawing at the walls, full of screaming voices. A window slammed. Glass shattered. Dust flew into Rose's eyes. The front door! She'd left it open.

But nothing could make her move from under that bed.

She clenched her eyes shut. She clamped her fists over her ears. Hot tears ran down her cheeks. She could feel Swiney's trembling body next to her. Rose opened her mouth and screamed with every ounce of strength.

But nothing could keep the roar of that wind from her ears. Something crashed inside the house. More hailstones drummed on the roof.

Then the rain came, in floods and torrents, lashing out of the sky, pounding on the roof. The roaring wind faded as quickly as it had come. Then there was only the sound of pouring rain. A fresh, cool breeze blew through the house.

Rose opened her eyes and stirred. She was afraid to come out. Swiney was still crying. She inched out from under the bed and peered around the bedroom. It looked the same as always, except that the chinking had fallen out of the log walls here and there and lay crumbled on the floor.

She craned to see through the door into the

kitchen. Shards of glass lay scattered on the floor.

Rose crawled out from under the bed and stood on quivery legs. She tiptoed into the kitchen. The window had shattered and hung crazily from one hinge. The curtain was all tangled up and torn. A chair lay on its side. The table had skidded across the room. The lamp had tipped over on it, and coal oil dripped onto the floor. Rose set it back up. Water splashed onto the stove from the pipe hole. The pipe was askew.

But the house was still standing.

"Rose, Swiney!" Papa's voice called out. Then the true horror of the storm came rushing at Rose. Effie and Mama and Abe. What had happened to them? And Fido and Blackfoot, and the colt and all the livestock!

"Papa!" Rose choked out through a fresh wave of tears. "Papa!" she screamed. She ran out onto the porch. Papa came hobbling across the soggy barnyard. He was all smeared with mud and soaking wet. His hat was gone.

Rose rushed into his arms, sobbing.

"All right, then," Papa said in a husky voice. "All right. Hush now. It's gone. Are you hurt anyplace?"

Rose shook her head.

"Swiney?"

"He's . . . in the . . . house." Rose hiccuped through her tears. "He's safe. . . . Oh, Papa . . . it was horrible!"

Then Rose wiped away her tears and looked around the farm. Big limbs and scraps of shattered trees lay everywhere on the ground. The barnyard was covered with the white dots of melting hailstones.

Something glittered by the barn, a jumble of dark wood. Rose looked closer. It was a smashed dresser. But sitting on top was the mirror without a single crack in it.

The stock barn, the dairy barn, and the house were all standing solid, except that some shingles were gone from all the roofs. The rails of the garden fence were scattered like bits of straw. The roof of the henhouse was completely gone, and Rose knew that some of the chickens must have been killed or blown away.

Cyclone!

Swiney stumbled out onto the porch, rubbing his eyes and snuffling up the last of his tears. He was shivering uncontrollably.

"It's a miracle," Papa said, shaking his head and hobbling toward the dairy barn.

"Papa, your foot!" Rose cried.

"It's all right, Rose," he said. "May threw me and ran off. The wind tore off one of my boots, is all. I'm fit as a fiddle."

"Is Mama all right?" Rose asked fearfully. "And Effie? And Abe?" There were so many people and animals to think of.

"Yes," said Papa, pulling a big branch down off the roof of the dairy barn. "Everyone is all right. The cyclone hopped right over the valley. It just barely missed us. I was riding home when it passed over. The thing just picked itself up and set itself down farther east. It's a plain miracle we weren't all blown away."

Swiney and Rose followed Papa around, careless of the pouring rain, as he inspected the house, the barns, and the henhouse. Some of the chickens were gone. Papa said they probably were sucked out when the roof blew away.

"If they weren't killed or carried too far off, I reckon they'll find their way home," he said hopefully.

Papa was looking at the stovepipe in the kitchen when Rose heard a strange yowling just under the splashing and pattering of rain.

"What the dickens?" Papa said in wonderment. They all went outside to hear better. They listened intently. Someone was crying nearby, but they couldn't tell where.

Then Swiney shouted. "Over there, Mr. Wilder! Look!"

He pointed up into a tall hickory tree behind the house, on the other side of the spring. Rose looked but she couldn't see anything at first. Then she spied a bundle of rags caught in some limbs. It moved!

"Why, that beats all!" Papa cried. "It sounds like a baby. Can you hear it?"

And then Rose did. There really was a baby in that tree, and it was crying its heart out.

They ran around the top of the spring, over the big rock, and looked up into the branches. It was hard to see through the leaves, but now the sound of that baby crying was as plain as anything.

"Stay here," Papa ordered. "You youngsters keep an eye on it, in case it falls. You might be able to catch it."

He dashed to the barn. Swiney and Rose stared into the trees, catching glimpses of the squirming bundle through the tree canopy. It was impossible to imagine—the cloud had plucked a baby up from another house and plopped it down right on Rocky Ridge Farm. And it was alive!

Papa came running back with rope and a sack. He shinnied up the trunk and picked his way among the branches until he reached the bundle of rags.

Then Papa's hearty laughter filtered down through the leaves. "Looks like it hasn't even got a scratch," he called down. He carefully put the baby in the sack, tied a rope around it, and gently let it down until Rose and Swiney could grab it.

They quickly untied the sack. The tiny baby shrieked even louder, waving its little fists, its face red and blotchy. Swiney helped Rose lay it gently down in the soft leaves. She cooed to it and held her apron over its face to keep off the rain. Papa scrambled down from the tree.

"I'd call any man a liar to his face if I didn't see it with my own eyes," he said, squatting by the swaddling baby and twisting an end of his mustache. The baby cried out in a mewling voice. "I've heard of it raining cats and dogs, but this is the first time it ever rained babies."

They all laughed, and the laughter felt as refreshing and pure in their throats as a drink of cool spring water on hot day of threshing. The baby stopped crying, surprised by the laughter. Its clear blue eyes gazed at Rose soberly, and it gurgled. Rose and Swiney and Papa looked at each other with shining eyes.

It was good to be alive.

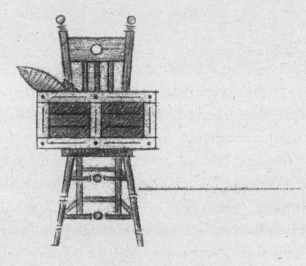

Cyclone Sally

"Where d'ya think she came from?" Swiney asked as Rose carried the baby into Mama and Papa's room. She laid her on the bed as carefully as an egg on a table, being extra careful to hold her head so it wouldn't flop.

Rose had taken off the baby girl's dirty, wet dress and wrapped her in one of Mama's old quilts. Papa was out checking the livestock.

Fido had finally slunk back into the barnyard from wherever he had hidden himself during the storm. Now he sat shivering at Rose's feet, leaning against her leg, panting.

He was still scared and wouldn't leave her side. Rose hadn't seen Blackfoot yet, or her kitten. But the cats liked to hide in the hayloft of the barn. She knew they must be all right.

"How can anyone say?" Rose finally said. She wondered how far the baby had flown. She wondered what that must be like, to fly through the air. She wished the baby could say.

"Her mama and papa must be terribly worried," Rose said. "But I'll take good care of her." Secretly, wickedly, the thought flickered through Rose's head that she would like that baby to stay right where it was, forever. Then she brushed the thought away, like a fly.

The baby squirmed and made a crooked face. Then she started to cry again.

"I think she's hungry," Rose decided. "Go fetch the milk jug out of the spring and let's give her some."

Rose fed the milk to her in a spoon. Most of it splashed down her chin. But she was very hungry, and every time Rose took the spoon away to get more, she wriggled helplessly, waving her hands and feet like an overturned bug.

"You're a born mother, Rose," Papa compli-
mented her. "Why don't you fold up a diaper
out of some flannel scraps? She's likely to river
herself and soil Mama's quilt. I'm going over to
Abe's place and see if I can catch May. If I can
I'll head into town and see if anybody's missing
a baby. I may be gone a good long spell, and
who can say when Mama might be back?"

Papa had milked the cows and settled the
livestock. Now it was up to Rose and Swiney
to take care of the farm.

"Yes, Papa. We will," Rose promised in her
most grown-up voice.

The rain clouds had cleared off, and the flaring sunset lit the kitchen with a golden light.
Then the light went out and the forest turned
dark. Rose brought the lamp into the bedroom,
and she and Swiney played with the little girl.
They let her tiny hands squeeze their fingers,
talked nonsense to her, and tickled her feet to
make her smile until they realized how hungry
they were.

Swiney made a fire in the fireplace, and Rose
cooked a supper of fried mush with gravy left

over from yesterday's dinner. They brought the baby into the kitchen and made a bed out of an old apple crate. They set the crate on a chair, and then sat down to eat, just like a natural family.

They ate ferociously until their hunger was blunted. All the time they watched the baby. She was very quiet now. She took a big breath and sighed. Her eyelids drooped, and she began a whispering snore.

Swiney took a long drink of water and burped.

"Just because the grown-ups are gone doesn't let you forget your manners," Rose scolded.

"Aw, heck. What's the difference?" Swiney scowled. He wiped his mouth with his sleeve and stared at his empty plate for a moment.

"Did you figure we was gonna be killed?" he said in a quiet voice.

"When?"

"When do you think, you old wet hen? The cyclone."

Rose got up and tucked the quilt closer around the baby's head. She couldn't stop fussing over her.

"No," she said when she was sure the covers were perfectly arranged. "I didn't think anything. I was too scared."

"Maybe some people died," said Swiney. "I'll just bet they did. That was some big wind. Maybe even that little girl's ma and pa died."

"Oh, I hope not," Rose said quickly, and she meant it with all her heart. But she couldn't help wondering, What if they did? Would Mama and Papa let the baby stay and live with them? If only they could keep her, Rose would care for her just as if she were her own real sister.

Suddenly she felt herself overflowing with tenderness. She bent down and brushed a feathery kiss on the little girl's cheek.

They gathered up the dirty dishes, and Swiney helped Rose wash and dry them. They tidied up the kitchen, wiped up the spilled coal oil, swept up the last bits of broken glass, and set the window back in its place.

Then they took the little girl out of the crate-bed and set her back on Mama and Papa's big bed. Rose and Swiney sat on either side of the baby and watched her sleep. Her mouth worked a little now and again, and she stretched once. But she slept as soundly as a log. Rose gently loosened her bonnet and lightly petted her wispy blond hair.

They talked a long time, about the storm, about Effie's baby, and even about Swiney's mother and father.

"I sure wish they'd of lived," he said mournfully. "Sometimes I think I 'member 'em, but I can't rightly say if it's me 'membering or somethin' Abe told me. It's like they were a dream, darn near real. And then I wake up and they're gone. I sure would've liked to see what they looked like."

He sighed heavily. "When I get to studying on it, it purely mixes me up."

Rose looked at the little girl, and every wish she had of keeping her flew out of her head. She said a silent prayer to herself that her poor mother and father would live and come to take her home where they could love her in that special way that Rose had always known.

They talked and watched the baby and

talked and watched. They made up a name for the little girl, even though they knew she had her own name. They called her Cyclone Sally.

Finally Rose's eyelids grew very heavy, and she laid her head down.

She woke once in the dark of the night. The lamp had sucked up all the oil and gone out. But in the dim moonlight coming from the kitchen, she could see Cyclone Sally's peaceful face, and Swiney snuggled up to her.

"Rose. Wake up, dear. Swiney, wake yourself up, son."

Rose blinked and squinted her eyes against the bright light of the lantern. Mama's drawn face leaned over and peered into the quilt.

"Oh, isn't she a darling," she crooned.

"She's a blamed amazement is what she is." Papa's soft voice came from behind Mama.

"Mama, are you all right?" Rose mumbled in her half-sleep. "Is Effie all right? Did the baby come?"

"The babies came, Rose. And everyone is just as safe and healthy as can be. The cyclone just missed Abe's house, too. I'm so glad you both are safe." She kissed Rose on the forehead.

Rose rubbed her eyes. Then they flew open. She sat up. "Babies?"

"Yes. Effie had twins. A little girl and a little boy. And now this baby drops from heaven. Seems as if babies are one crop that won't fail."

Rose jumped off the bed and hugged Mama. "Oh, Mama, it's wonderful." Two babies to spoil! Three! It was too much to be believed.

Now Swiney was up and blinking fast.

"Granny Albers catched *two* babies! Golly, no wonder Effie was so fat. That's the best! I'm a-going to go see 'em!"

"Me too!" Rose shouted. Mama shushed her, but the baby shrieked in surprise, and began to cry and fret.

"Maybe she's hungry again," guessed Rose.

"You mustn't visit with Effie just yet," Mama said wearily. "She must lie in for a good long spell and gather back her strength. Mrs. Stubbins will stay with her, and Abe is there to help as well. Effie needs to rest. And so do I." With a little groan, she sank down on the bed beside the baby and peered in the covers at her.

"She looks a little like you did," Mama said. "You were a good howler, too."

The baby was crying steadily now. Swiney dashed out to get the milk jug. Papa fixed the stovepipe, and Rose made a fire in the stove to heat some water. Mama began to change the baby's diaper.

"Did Papa find its mother and father?" Rose called from the kitchen.

"Mr. Cooley heard at the depot that some folks over at Cedar Gap maybe lost a child in the cyclone. Imagine that. It's near ten miles from here. I can't see how a baby could fly so far, without a single bump. The things she must have seen!"

Mama and Rose took turns feeding the baby while the water warmed in the stove reservoir. The first fingers of gray light crept into the yard, and the day birds began to chirp and twitter. A mockingbird, the same one that came back every spring, sang its heart out from the chimney. The little house filled with its cheerful music.

A gentle, fresh breeze blew in through the

door and windows. It was a new day, and every-thing seemed new to Rose. She saw and felt everything as if it were the first time.

When the water was warm she carefully car-ried the washpan into the bedroom and then brought the jar of soft soap.

Mama showed Rose how to wash and change the baby.

"Did anyone die in the cyclone?" Rose wanted to know. "I saw two cows flying in the air. And someone's dresser landed by the barn. It was smashed to pieces, but the mirror wasn't even cracked."

"Papa said some people were hurt, and there may have been a death. Make sure you don't get the soap in her eyes, now.

"Some livestock was killed, but it missed the town, thank goodness. You never can tell which way luck will run. Well, she's all fed and bathed. Let's wrap her up nice and snug and take her in the kitchen while we fix break-fast."

Everyone had stories to tell while they ate. Papa said he'd found a big nail driven deep by the wind into the trunk of a stout ash tree in the timber lot. Swiney had found bits of broken china, and a shoe that wasn't Papa's.

Mama said she and Mrs. Stubbins had put Effie on the floor, so she wouldn't fall out of bed in the storm and hurt herself. Then they huddled down on the floor beside her. "But that old Granny Albers just sat there in a chair, smoking her pipe, as peaceful and alert as a mother bird on its nest. It was almost as if she knew she could make that storm pass us by."

After the cyclone had hopped over Rocky Ridge Farm, its hungry tentacle had touched down in Macomb, the town where the desperados had robbed the train.

"They say it tore up the place pretty bad," Papa said. "About all that's standing are the well pumps and some chimneys. A bunch of folks from town took the train over there to help out, and tend the wounded."

"Those poor people," Mama said. "To think that it might just have easily been us."

They all ate in silence for a moment, thinking grateful thoughts.

"I haven't even had time to look," Mama finally said. "How are the crops? Is the garden gone?"

"We took our lumps," said Papa, refilling his cup from the coffee pot. "There's a fair piece of mending on the roofs. The worst is that we lost part of the orchard."

Rose's stomach flopped. The orchard! She'd forgotten all about it. The apple trees were more important than almost anything on the farm.

"How much?" Mama asked.

"I reckon a third of the trees won't make it to next spring. Now don't you worry yourself, Rose. We've got through worse scrapes than this. And the rest of the trees are in fine shape."

"And the corn?" Mama asked anxiously.

"It broke some of the stalks, but not so many. Long as the moisture holds out, we should get by next winter, or maybe buy a few bushels.

"The garden got stirred up some, and the fence needs mending. But most of the plants are still there. I'd say we've had our task set before us."

"Yes, and after losing so many chickens, too," Mama sighed.

With that, they all went to work. There was no time to give to the simple joy of being alive. To breathe, to see light again, to feel the sun on their faces, was a great blessing .

But there was too much to do even to stop and thank God for life, for safety, one another, and the babies. The cyclone had spared them, but the roaring black cloud had left a wreck of things.

Home Folks

The next morning before breakfast, a young man with a bandaged arm and a woman with a cut over her eye drove into the barnyard. The backrest was broken off the seat of their wagon, and one of the wheels wobbled. They were Cyclone Sally's mother and father. The mother cried and cried when Mama gently put the little girl in her arms. Rose watched with a mix of joy and sadness.

They said they were Mr. and Mrs. Kirby, and Sally's real name was Mamie. Their farm was near Cedar Gap, west of Mansfield. Mamie was just six months old, and she was their first child.

Mrs. Kirby was standing in their yard, bewitched by the cyclone, when it struck. Mamie flew right out of her arms. The wind threw Mr. Kirby against a tree, and a stick of flying wood hit Mrs. Kirby in the head.

"It came up so fast, it just about mixed up the days of the week," Mr. Kirby said. "We don't know how we could ever thank you. The storm ruined our farm. Picked up the whole house and turned it upside down. Killed most of my stock, too, and tore up the fields. Mamie's 'bout all we got left."

The Kirbys stayed for coffee. Mrs. Kirby never stopped rocking Mamie, and kissing and fussing over her. When she wasn't crying, she was sniffling and getting ready to cry.

"We've got a heap of work to do on the place," Mr. Kirby said. "Might as well say we're starting over from today."

"It was a pleasure to care for Mamie," said Mama. "She is a darling little girl and you are welcome in our home anytime."

"But next time," Papa chimed in, "it might be safer if you all came in through the front door."

Everyone laughed. Even Mrs. Kirby managed a thin smile through her tears.

Mama, Papa, Rose, and Swiney stood on the porch and watched them drive away. They were all quiet, listening to the wagon rumble across the bridge and start along the creek toward town. That little girl would always be Cyclone Sally to Rose, and she would never forget her as long as she lived.

Now they rushed to clean up and catch up. On top of the regular summer chores there were repairs to the roofs, the garden fence to be fixed so the woods creatures wouldn't eat up the vegetables, crops to be replanted, windows to be repaired, and a cyclone cellar to be dug.

"Once burned, twice shy," Papa said. "I won't hand fate a second chance to get at us."

He dug a pit near the henhouse, not even deep enough to stand in, The ground was too rocky to dig deeper. Then he mounded the dirt and stones around three sides of it and built a slanting log roof over the opening.

The roof had a small door in the middle, on

leather hinges. Rose climbed inside. It was crowded and stuffy in there, and very dark when the door was closed. Papa showed her how to lock the crossbar in place so nothing could pull that door open.

"If a cyclone ever comes again," he told her, "you run and hide from it in this cellar, not under the bed."

Paul and George Cooley came out from town almost every day to help. They worked as well as any one of them and hardly complained at all, even when the midday sun beat mercilessly on their necks. Mr. and Mrs. Cooley helped as often as they could get away from their own chores.

Rose could not keep her grateful feeling about the storm when she walked through the orchard and saw so many of the trees snapped in half. The poor leaves were turning yellow and curling as they slowly died. Papa pruned them back. He said the stunted trunks would put out new shoots next year. But those trees would not bear fruit for a long time.

Rose hated that cyclone for hurting their future.

———

Rose had to wait a whole week to see Effie and the babies. The weather stayed stifling hot and dry as bleached bones. The parched ground had drunk up the rain brought by the cyclone and was thirsty as ever. Papa said that Ozark soil was so stony it couldn't hold on to the water. It drained right away.

On Sunday, the family finally went to visit the Bairds. Effie lay in bed with a bundle tucked on either side of her. She let Rose hold each of them. The babies were much smaller than Cyclone Sally, delicate as the petals of violets and pink as newborn mice.

Rose carried the boy by the window to see him better. He squinted at the light and squirmed. His mouth made a hard little circle.

"What's his name?" Rose asked.

"That there is James," said Effie, plumping up her pillow. "And this one here is Elza. Them was the names of Abe's ma and pa."

Abe stood proudly by, a grin on his face, bashfully rocking from foot to foot. Mrs. Stubbins bustled and clattered about the stove, getting up a pot of tea. Mama and Papa sat at the little table, chatting with Abe and Mrs. Stubbins. Rose and Swiney hovered around Effie and the babies.

Elza had a tiny curl of brown hair in the middle of her head, and she was even smaller than James. They were very quiet babies, squirming and wriggling but never crying out. Their faces moved at times as if they were asking a question.

Swiney plumped himself down on the bed at Effie's feet. He was as restless as a boy about to go fishing.

"They're really somethin', ain't they, Rose?" he crowed, bouncing up and down. "I'm a uncle, now. Imagine that. They got to call me Uncle Swiney." Then he laughed and threw himself back on the bed.

"You be still, Uncle Swiney, or I'll jerk a knot in your tail," Effie scolded. "You'll give the little 'uns a fright with all your commotion."

Mama traded garden tips with Mrs. Stubbins and Papa and Abe talked about crops. The hot sun was starting to hurt the corn, Abe said. Rose's ears pricked up.

"Them leaves is a-starting to twist and turn," he said. "Iffen we don't see some proper rain soon, we're a-gonna be up agin it come next winter."

"I'm sure the rain will come," Mama said hopefully. "With all the springs here that run even in the dry weather, I should think a bad drought would be uncommon."

"We've had our share of poor luck," Mrs. Stubbins said. "There's been years we was purely under the lion's paw, and nary thing to be done for it. But we ain't had a bad drought for a long spell."

"Nothing could ever be as rough as what we fought against in the Dakotas, before we came here," said Papa. "Seven years and not a good one among them. Things'd have to go mighty sour to break our spirit."

The corn was almost laid by now. The hoeing had been dusty work, but all the good straight rows were clean and tidy. The corn rustled and fluttered gaily in the oveny breezes, but the leaves were beginning to pale and curl. Here and there Rose found cracks in the soil, and little bowl-shaped places where birds had taken their dust baths.

One day when Papa came home from an errand in town, he rushed into the kitchen excitedly waving a letter.

"Great news!" he shouted. "Father and Mother are coming for a visit."

"My, we haven't seen them in . . . how long has it been? Almost six years, I should think," said Mama. "Are they coming all this way just to visit us?"

Rose knew she had met Grandpa and Grandma Wilder because Mama and Papa had told her so. But she couldn't remember them.

"They're on their way to Louisiana," Papa said as he washed his hands for supper. He came to the table with a bounce in his step.

"Gosh, it'll be just grand to see them again." He shook the letter open with a little snap. "Listen to this, Bess. Father says he's sold out his place up in Minnesota. I'll bet he got a pretty price for it, too. He always was the clever one at showing a good gain.

"He's going to visit my brother Perley and my sister Eliza Jane, in Crowley."

"Where's that?" Rose asked.

"It's a town on the Gulf of Mexico, in rice country. Your uncle Perley and aunt 'Liza moved down there last year. Father's looking for a new place to plunk his money.

"I'll just bet Eliza Jane's got it all figured for Mother and Father to move to Louisiana. But maybe he'll settle right here, in Mansfield. Jiminy, I wish we'd get some rain to green up the place, Bess. I'd hate for Father to see everything looking poorly."

The little house was too small for Grandpa and Grandma Wilder to stay on Rocky Ridge Farm. Grandpa wrote that Papa should find them a place to board. Mr. and Mrs. Cooley had one of their extra rooms to let, so Papa fixed it that they would stay in town with them.

Papa worked extra hard in the next weeks to put the farm in apple-pie order. He fixed every fence, whitewashed the henhouse, and worked until after dark in the barn putting a fresh coat of shiny black paint on the wagon.

He came in each night droop-shouldered, mumbled good night, and practically fell asleep taking off his shoes. But then he was up early the next morning, at it again, fixing the hinge on the barn door, replacing the cracked step board on the front porch.

One night at supper, the heat from the cookstove made the kitchen extra sticky and uncomfortable. Papa's head nodded, and he nearly drifted off to sleep over his food.

"Manly, you're running yourself ragged," Mama said worriedly. "There's no sense making yourself sick. You don't have to showboat for your own home folks."

"Got to put a good face on the farm," Papa muttered, rubbing his face and yawning hard. "Father's a rich, successful farmer. Don't want him to think we're living like sharecroppers."

"Well, enough is enough, Manly. The best face you can put on it won't make a silk purse out of a sow's ear. Father Wilder will see what he sees, and nothing more. And if he's any kind of man, he'll be proud of what we've built."

Finally, one day Papa took the mares to

town, rented the finest buggy he could get from the livery, and fetched Grandma and Grandpa Wilder from the depot.

Rose and Mama had gotten up very early, scrubbing the house until it shone.

Rose stood on the porch in her Sunday dress and greased shoes. She was a little bit nervous. They had never had such important company. She wanted to make Papa proud.

Grandpa Wilder was very old. He carried a gold-headed cane and moved as slowly as a tortoise getting down from the buggy. A black derby sat on his bald head. He wore a fine, crisply pressed dark suit with a boiled collar and a gold watch chain draped across his bulgy stomach. Rose thought he looked like a newspaper drawing of a president. He smiled politely, and Rose curtsied back to him.

Grandma was also very old, and small. But she was quick and fluttery and plump like a well-fed sparrow. She could never be still.

Her beautiful lawn dress had a high collar of the most delicate crochet, and she carried a fringed white parasol. On top of her big puff of snow-white hair, which she had twisted into a knot, she wore a wide-brimmed hat decorated with colorful bits of calico.

Her eyes danced and her hands moved as she looked about and remarked on the farm. "This is a lovely setting, Almanzo. The hills here are so restful to look at."

Rose held out her hand to shake. "Hello, Grandmother Wilder," she said in her most polite voice. "I'm pleased you've come."

"Oh, child!" she burbled. She gathered Rose up in a tender hug that smelled of lilacs. Then she held her by the shoulders and looked Rose up and down with smiling eyes. "Let me get a proper look. Yes, I suspected so. What a beautiful little girl you've become. Such clear, bright eyes, and beautiful long hair.

"I so miss having my grandchildren about to spoil. I don't know why my brood had to up and scatter themselves to the four winds the way they did. Shame on you, Manzo, for keeping an old woman from the simple joys of her old age."

Papa grinned and jammed his hands in his

suit pockets like a shy schoolboy.

Grandpa and Grandma Wilder took most of their meals with the Cooleys, and visited every day at the farm for dinner. Papa spent hours walking slowly over the farm with Grandpa. Their heads bent together, they discussed crops and weather and prices.

Some days Papa took the grown-ups for a buggy ride around the hills, to see the countryside and look at other farms. Papa said Grandpa was thinking of buying some land in Missouri.

One day they rented a big hack and drove to Hartville for a picnic on the Gasconade River. Rose went swimming in the dark cool water, and after a delicious dinner of fried chicken and cold roasted potatoes, they ate their fill of watermelon.

On the way back they stopped at the Cooleys' house to leave off Grandma and Grandpa. All along the streets of the town the people sat on their porches and in their front yards, trying to keep cool in the warm evening.

Papa was helping Grandpa Wilder down

from the buggy when George came shuffling out of the house, his face downcast. He opened the gate and looked up at them with bleary eyes. His mouth wobbled and his fists were clenched.

"Why George, what's the matter?" Mama asked.

A sob tore from his throat. "It's Pa, Mrs. Wilder," his tortured voice croaked. "He's been killed."

A Sea of Grief

Rose stood close by Papa as they waited on the depot platform. The wild, lonely cry of the whistle floated to them on the early evening breeze. The train would be pulling in in a few minutes. Papa sighed heavily.

Two men hauled a trunk across the platform and set it gently down next to a cluster of milk cans. A small crowd of passengers began to drift out of the waiting room, stealing glances at Mrs. Cooley and speaking in hushed voices. From inside the depot Rose heard the clicking of the telegraph. Two men in black suits and black hats stood smoking cigars by a shiny black hack with a roof and cloth sides.

Mama sat with Mrs. Cooley on a bench by the waiting room door. Mrs. Cooley lifted her black veil to dab at her eyes with her handkerchief. Paul and George waited by an empty freight wagon in their Sunday best, silent and sober, with faraway looks in their eyes.

The words crashed again and again in Rose's ears like a thunderclap. Mr. Cooley was dead. He was killed in a train wreck on a railroad errand to West Plains. She shivered when she remembered Papa's strangled cry when he heard the news. Mr. Cooley had been his closest friend.

The Cooleys had come with Rose's family all that way from South Dakota, to escape a terrible drought and to start a new life, and now that life was finished for Mr. Cooley. He would never come to Rocky Ridge Farm again and talk with Papa about the future of the country, and the boom in Mansfield.

Rose had desperately wanted to cry. Poor Paul and George left with no father, poor Mrs. Cooley a widow.

At the Cooleys' house, Mama had told Rose to wait while the grown-ups went inside to see to Mrs. Cooley. Rose had wandered around the outside of the big white house, hoping to hear something. She peered around the back corner and spotted Paul, crouched beside the back door, crying noiselessly. That was a fearful sight. He clenched his teeth so hard his jaw bulged. His smooth face seemed turned to stone, and big tears rolled out of his dark eyes. But he never made a sound.

Rose had tiptoed back to the hack to wait. She wanted to cry, but she couldn't bring a single tear. She felt miserably sad, but mostly she was scared. She couldn't stop herself from worrying about Papa, and about Mama, too. She could never imagine being without either of them.

Now, standing on the wooden platform waiting for Mr. Cooley's body to come home, Rose sidled close to Papa and slipped her hand into his. Papa squeezed back, and stared blankly down the track.

A plume of black smoke unfurled over the

horizon and then the engine appeared down the tracks, coming around the bend. Rose's heart began to pound. The bell clanged as the engine slowly drew to a stop with a squeal and a shudder. A great cloud of steam blew out from under it. The iron wheels crackled as they cooled, and the locomotive panted huskily, like an exhausted animal catching its breath. People began to stream off the train.

Now the Cooleys and Wilders moved down the platform to the baggage car. Some men dressed all in black came with them. They were the undertakers. Everyone waited in a somber group as a swirl of passengers and bags and trunks sorted themselves out. Finally all the bags had been unloaded, and a long box of bright new wood poked out of the baggage car.

Papa, the two undertakers, and two other men helped lift it and gently set it onto a baggage wagon. Then they rolled it slowly down the platform. Mrs. Cooley walked behind with George and Paul by her side. Rose took Mama's hand and walked behind them, staring at Mrs. Cooley's black hem as it swept the boards. It seemed there was nothing to say and no one to say it to. Rose felt small and alone, an island of sadness floating in a sea of grief.

It was hard to find something to be glad about after that. They had gone to the cemetery and buried Mr. Cooley. "Ashes to ashes, and dust to dust," the minister had said. Rose had shuddered as Papa and the other men lowered the box into the ground.

Then everyone went back to the Cooleys' house where Grandma Wilder and some women from town had helped make a meal. That day had been a blur of black cloth, long faces, and trembling silences.

Grandma and Grandpa Wilder stayed a little while in Mansfield after that, but their visit had lost its pleasure. The day before they left, at supper on the farm, Grandpa Wilder cleared his throat and made a surprising announcement in his deep, sober voice.

"Mrs. Cooley tells me she aims to sell the place. Says it's too much to keep up on her own. So I've made an offer."

"You're buying the Cooleys' house?" Papa asked in astonishment. "I thought you might buy some farmland, Father. Something that could be built up."

"I've looked this country over," Grandpa said; "I don't like to take a thing from the hard work you've put into this place, son, but farming these rocky hills is an uphill fight.

"I've had a letter from your sister and brother in Louisiana. They write that the country there is wide open and mighty fertile, with constant water. The town is bustling. Why, there are seven depots in Crowley and a big market for rice. A smart fellow could double his money in a few years.

"But I'm not going to be in this world much longer," he continued.

"Oh, James!" Grandma Wilder interrupted. "I wish you wouldn't speak so, and in front of Rose."

Papa stirred uneasily in his chair. Mama stared at her plate.

"It's a fact of life," Grandpa said. "I'm an old man and I won't walk this earth forever. So I'm going to put the house in your name, to do with as you see fit. Consider it part of my bequest to you, son."

Papa was silent for a long moment, twisting an end of his mustache. He looked at Mama, at Grandma, and finally back at Grandpa.

"Thank you, Father," he finally said. "But what would I do with a house? We have the farm. We live here."

"Rent it out, of course," Grandpa said. "In a stretch of hard sledding, the extra money would be useful. And someday, when you may want to sell it, the value will have increased."

And so it was settled. Mama and Papa would own the Cooleys' house and Mrs. Cooley would live there until she had decided what to do. Mama said Mrs. Cooley thought to move back East, to be near her relatives. Rose prayed hard that she wouldn't. Paul and George were her oldest friends. She couldn't imagine them ever not living close enough for Sunday visits, or not being in school with her. That was something she could cry about.

———

They drove back to the depot a second time, to say good-bye to Grandma and Grandpa Wilder. Grandma cried, and Papa's voice was husky when he said his final good-bye and shook Grandpa's hand.

"Remember what I've said," Grandpa told Papa. "If you folks want to try your hand at rice farming, just send word and come on down."

"Thank you, Father. But we're settled here now, and we have to finish what we've started."

The conductor cried out, "All aboard!" They climbed up into the car and Grandma waved her handkerchief from the window as the train belched and stuttered on its way.

And then they were gone. Papa stood a long time watching the train as it rolled faster and faster down the track, a pall of black smoke billowing after it. Then the last car rounded the bend and disappeared.

Catching Sunlight

Days on Rocky Ridge Farm returned to the cozy rhythms of everyday life. Things were the same, but they were altogether different, too. As often as she could, Rose visited the Bairds, to help Effie with her chores and to play with James and Elza. The babies were growing fast, and Rose could never spend enough time feeding them, and cleaning them, and tickling their tiny little feet to make them smile and squirm.

Paul and George came more often to visit, but they were not so playful as before. When they played Fox and Geese, George would forget his moves and make foolish mistakes. When he lost, he would stalk off and sulk on a stump behind the barn.

Paul talked earnestly in his deepening voice of the telegrapher's position he would find when he finished school, of how he would take care of his mother and George. Before her very eyes, Paul was becoming a man, and that made Rose feel a bit childish. She missed the lighthearted adventures they used to have, exploring Williams Cave or looking for Indian arrowheads along Fry Creek.

It had been such a long time ago that they were a little girl and a little boy playing Tag or Blindman's Buff in the yard outside Grandma and Grandpa Ingalls' house in South Dakota. They were always changing, all the time, and now the change was coming fast.

Rose noticed it inside herself, too. She was growing bigger. Mama had had to let out the hem of her best dress twice since last spring. Even her thoughts were getting bigger. She never played with her dolls anymore. They lay lonely and forgotten in the drawers of her dresser.

Instead she lived in the world of the books she read and in her imagination about the real world beyond the gentle hills. She knew the joy of mothering a little baby, and she had felt the heavy weight of grief. She had begun to speak her mind and learned to hold her tongue. And yet, the more grown-up she became and the more she understood life's secrets, the more she yearned to know.

The dry days of that summer piled one atop the other. One day while Papa was plowing the corn for the last time, the mules ran off toward the creek, dragging the plow with them. They dragged the plow across the rows of corn, bolted right through the fence, through the brush and trees, and down the bank until they splashed into the shallow, scummy water.

None of Papa's hollering could make them move until they had drunk their fill, were cooled off, and had decided to go back to work.

One evening at supper Mama asked Papa, "Why didn't you turn the cows and horses out today? They were bawling all afternoon.

Seems a pity to keep them shut up, off the pastures."

"I guess maybe I turned them out a little too soon this summer," Papa said. "I was cutting it a little close, to save buying feed. Didn't let the grass get a fair start. And with this dry weather, it won't do them any harm to eat dry feed a little longer. I'm going to tell you something, Bess. You make the kind of rhubarb pie my mother never dreamed of."

"Manly, we need rain, don't we? We need it badly. The garden is burning up."

"Well, the pastures need it pretty bad, yes. But we ought to get a shower any day now. I noticed a minute ago, it's clouding up in the west."

After she had rinsed the milk strainer and washed the pails, Rose went out into the yard. The night air was cool and sweet. Here and there fireflies flickered. The sky overhead was clear and full of stars, but there did seem to be a haziness over the western hills. It might rain before morning. No one could tell.

But the next morning the sun rose in a

cloudless sky, and all day long the sharp shadows of trees and buildings passed slowly from west to east. Fluffy white clouds sailed high in the blueness overhead, and their shadows followed them across the blossoming fields.

All the earth was a riot of blooms. Meadows and pastures were masses of white and blue, purple and gold. Daisies and foxglove and wild larkspur were taking the fields. Dandelions by the thousands appeared in the pastures and in a day had turned to seedballs.

Papa brought fistfuls of flowers in every evening. The bouquets were beautiful, but Papa said all those weedy flowers were choking the crops, and the cow's milk was bitter from eating them.

"I best keep Bunting in the barn lot, so her milk will stay sweet," he said.

Some days at sunset there was a mackerel sky. Then all night long, even in her sleep, Rose waited for the sound of raindrops. Once a furious wind arose, shaking the little house, slamming doors, filling the darkness outside with the roaring of treetops.

Rose dashed down the stairs with her heart pounding in her chest. She could not hear the wind without thinking of the cyclone.

Mama was stumbling against the furniture, hurrying to close the windows.

"It's all right, Rose," Mama said. "Just a windstorm. Maybe we'll finally get some rain."

The gale at the windows had been hot, and blowing dust. But then the first large raindrops spattered on the roof. Rose looked at Papa in the dim lamplight. He was sitting on the edge of the bed, listening. The sharp shadows on his face softened. He smiled at her. It seemed a long time since Rose had seen him smile so easily.

The sound of raindrops was followed by a gust of air, then there was only the sound of the wind, a rumbling of thunder, now and then a lightning flash. But no more rain fell. In the morning, the little spats of wet in the dust of the garden were already dried.

After breakfast Papa set to tinkering with the cultivator. Behind the blades he fastened a long stick, crosswise, and to that stick he fastened loops of heavy chain, one inside another.

"They'll drag behind, and pack the soil," Papa explained.

"Why?" Rose asked.

"Packed ground holds the moisture."

"Are you going to drag it on the potatoes?"

"Maybe," he said. Then he chirruped to the mules and started out to the cornfield, the chain clinking musically behind.

Except for the rows of sweet corn, the garden was clean of weeds. Rose and Mama had pulverized every inch of soil. It lay smooth and gray as ashes and above it the air wavered in the throbbing heat.

Rose looked around the garden and for the first time she saw what the heat was doing. The tomatoes and the peas and the beans looked limp. Carrot tops and beet leaves were wilting. The carrots had become so bound in the earth that nothing could budge them.

The lettuce lay flat on the hot soil. The late-planted seeds baked without even sprouting. The dark green clumps of the potato leaves seemed to be panting for coolness in the vibrating air. Here and there a leaf was withered, turning brown.

In the pools along Fry Creek the backs of the perch stuck out above the water, making them fair game for snakes and raccoons. The drying-up creek was a somber place, even scary. Rose worried. If the water left, what might go next?

As tough-footed as she was from going barefoot all summer, Rose had to run mincing on the hot earth from shady spot to shady spot. The grass crackled underfoot. The sun poured down out of the pitiless sky. Papa led the cows and horses and mules, moving thin and listless, to the scummy creek to pluck the cropped grass from the edges.

Rose was hoeing the potatoes and knelt to look at them. She dug into one of the hills and pulled out a small, withered potato. She took it in her fingers and looked—a tiny pale nut, withered and hard. She flung it away and stood up, hot, dirty, and angry. She struck the hoe into the soil, struck deeper and deeper. But it was hard and dry, dry as ashes. Four inches down, there was only the first faint darkness that told of moisture.

Why didn't it rain? Nothing seemed to care about the garden or the fields. Not the hot earth under her feet, nor the great bright sky above. The careless, stubborn sun was turning all their work to dust. A little rain, just a little rain, was all they wanted. But it made no difference what they wanted, or how hard they worked for it. There was not a cloud in the sky.

When he came in from unhitching the horses at noon, Papa paused on the doorstep to wipe the trickling sweat from his forehead on his shirtsleeve. His parched red face was grimy with dust, his hat stained dark with sweat.

"Well, the earth is packed smooth between all the rows. That ought to hold the moisture, if anything would," he said wearily. "But if it doesn't rain soon, the meadows will be done for. The hay will go weedy."

Mama hardly looked up from the stove. Her mouth was a thin line, her forehead knotted in thought.

That night was beautiful, full of moonlight. The country was so still, so lovely with its curves of hills and masses of trees. In the dark it almost seemed to Rose that the daytime, with its hot sun and dusty earth, was a bad dream that would go away when she woke up. But each new day was like the last.

"I'm going to save the garden, anyway, if it kills me," Mama said the next morning. "Finish your breakfast, Rose. We've got work to do."

They went to work, drawing water from the spring, lugging pailfuls to the garden and going up and down the rows, stooping, giving a little to the roots of each plant. It was hard, back-breaking work, but it must be done. It scared Rose to see the garden dying. Each plant was like the baby birds Rose had once tried to save, withering away before her very eyes and nothing to be done about it.

"Ain't seen a season like it in a coon's age," Mr. Stubbins said one Sunday when he came by with Mrs. Stubbins and Alva to visit. He was leaning against the horse-lot gate talking to Mama and Papa.

"My oats don't look like they'd be worth a-cutting. As for the pastures, I'm a-feeding twelve head on hay at two dollars a ton. It's a-going to be hard for us all, if it don't rain right quick."

"It's the awful uncertainty," Mama said. "One good soaking rain might save things yet. I've cultivated and cultivated, and dust-mulched, trying to hang on to what we've got, just keeping the crops alive, praying for rain."

"Farming's no job for the faint of heart," Papa said. "You got to take the ups and downs in this business, I reckon."

If it would only rain, Papa said, the second hay crop might be saved. Some of the corn might live. If it would just rain!

That night Rose lay in bed in the stuffy house, tense, listening for wind, thunder, rain. In the morning there were clouds to the west. Great soft masses of gray rolled up into the blue. The air was heavy and still.

Rose's dress was wet through with sweat as she and Mama brought more pails of water and dribbled them on the garden rows. By midmorning the shadow of clouds was over the farm, but the breathless heat increased.

Rose kept looking up at the sky, hoping and waiting and worrying. Every little leaf, every grass stem, waited, panting, thirsting for the rain. The sullen dark gray clouds, heavy with rain, moved jaggedly upon each other, rumbling as though they were enormous boulders, rolling there together in the sky.

Then suddenly the thick hot air was pierced by little cool breezes, breaths of sweet, cool air carrying the smell of rain. Mama and Rose shot a glance at each other. Then they looked toward the cornfield where Papa was plowing. He was looking at them, too.

Papa tore the hat from his head and waved it. He shouted. They gazed up at the clouds, waiting. It was raining, in the west! Below the clouds hung a smooth gray curtain of rain. The wind was rising. Rose's skirt slapped around her knees. A large, warm drop fell on her forehead.

"It's coming!" Rose shouted, and she laughed. She ran inside to get a bucket and put it out in the yard. A fierce wind whipped her clothes. Rose wanted to run and shriek, to have wings like the swooping crows fleeing the coming storm.

"That's a good idea," Mama said. "Bring up the tubs. It's coming, all right. It's here." The first drops fell, hard-splashing and wide apart. There was a wonderful brightness on Mama's face, a light shining in it, as she stood there with buckets in her hands.

But still they stood in sunshine. Above the trees the sky was clear and blue. Then the soft clouds began to roll back from the blueness. Mama's shoulders sagged, and Rose felt a sob snag in her throat.

The great fluffy masses, white as cotton, rolled over each other, slowly and gracefully, as though playing. Wisps of white detached themselves and floated and melted in the widening sunshine.

Now enormous stretchs of sky were clean as glass, as after a thunderstorm. The thunder sounded a long way off, almost unheard. In no time there was only the merciless sun staring down, and the blue sky, smiling carelessly. Nothing had changed.

Rose turned the bucket upside down and sat on it. Papa came up from the field for a drink of water.

"Well, looked for while like we'd get a shower, didn't it," he said heartily, trying to fill the hollowness inside of them. "What are the tubs for?"

"To catch sunlight in," said Mama. She smiled thinly, but none of them laughed.

"Better luck next time," Papa said.

Dinner was not very good. The old potatoes were limp and soggy, the biscuits had been made with skimmed milk, and there was no pie. They were out of molasses, and pies took so much sugar. After they ate, Papa went back to work. He began cultivating the potatoes, using the chains. Many of the lower leaves were brown now.

Bunting came back from watering at the creek that night, sick and staggering. Papa said she must have eaten some weed that poisoned her. He did not feed her. She would have to be watched. They couldn't lose the cow.

That night Rose woke from a fitful sleep to the sound of voices. Mama and Papa were talking outdoors.

"What are you doing?" Papa's deep voice asked.

"Watering the garden."

Papa said something Rose couldn't hear. Then he raised his voice. "I won't have you working like this, you hear? In the middle of the night! Go on to bed, Bess, and get some rest."

The next day there were clouds in the south, but they sailed past, high overhead. By evening they had gathered low in the north, with mutterings of thunder and lightning flashes. That night there was again a tantalizing smell of rain in the air.

Then there were two days of low, gray sky. The leaves of the young apple trees hung limp, as though they too had given up hope. Papa said their roots were deep enough to survive any drought, but Rose worried just the same.

It had been dry so long now that Rose could

scarcely remember a time when it wasn't. Every day was the same. Overhead the sky hung gray with its withheld rain. It seemed deliberate in its hatefulness, smiling in its cruelty. The rain was there, and the sky held it and did not spill so much as a drop.

Fire!

The next day the sunset was a riot of purple, rose and gold, of streaks of pure green and shafts of sunlight. In the morning all the clouds were gone; only the clear blue remained, arching over the dying earth.

Somehow, miraculously, the spring continued to flow, although much slower now. Rose was helping Mama haul water for the garden when a beautiful buggy pulled by a sleek team rattled up the hill.

Mrs. Coday was driving, and another woman was with her. Both of them were dressed all in white, with white gloves and fancy-trimmed hats. The harness was black polished leather, studded with brass buttons. The beautiful buggy was painted dark green with all the trim painted orange-red.

Rose and Mama looked at each other, and Mama sighed. Their gingham dresses were limp, and stained at the hems with splashed water and settled dust. There was almost nothing in the house to offer visitors if they stayed to supper.

"We were just passing by, Mrs. Wilder, and I was saying to my sister Myrtle how yours is one of the tidiest little farms around these parts and she really ought to see it. I hope you don't mind."

"No, of course," Mama said pleasantly.

She brought chairs out on the porch. The two women looked like angels dressed in their airy dresses and broad hats. It felt strange to Rose to be sitting and visiting pleasantly while all around the whole earth was dying of thirst. They ought to be hauling water.

"May I get you a drink?" Mama asked.

"Yes, that would be pleasant," Mrs. Coday said.

Rose drew a pail of cool water from the spring. Mama brought out glasses, and they drank, sipping daintily.

"How charming it must be, living in the country!" Mrs. Coday's sister said brightly. She spoke in a crisp, proper voice that was refreshing to listen to.

"Yes," said Mama. "We like it."

"It's so beautiful, all the flowers. It seems to me I've never seen so many flowers. All the fields are simply gorgeous with so many colors. That one over there, just look at it."

Mama looked. It was the meadow where the weeds had smothered the alfalfa.

"It has been a very good year for flowers," Mama said.

"But I suppose," Mrs. Coday said, "farm people get so used to all this loveliness. Perhaps they . . . you hardly get the pleasure out of it that we do, being in the country just for the day."

"Perhaps," Mama said softly.

Mrs. Coday's sister looked up at the sky. "Dear me," she said suddenly. "It's getting cloudy! Oh, you don't think it's going to rain, do you? I hate to drive in the rain, and the buggy with no top, too."

The sultry sky was thickening again. The trees and the fields and the parched scanty grass of the barnyard were helpless under the heat that the remorseless sky pressed down upon them.

"Oh, no, I don't think it's going to rain," Mama assured them.

Finally, after what seemed an eternity to Rose, they thanked Mama for the water, and drove away.

"Let's get back to work," Mama said as soon as they were gone. They picked up their buckets and were about to walk down to the spring when Mama stopped suddenly, raising her face to the sky. She sniffed. At that same instant Rose's nostrils filled with a faint acrid smell that made her scalp crinkle with fear. Smoke!

"Who would be so careless as to start a fire in this weather?" Mama said. They scanned the sky, but they could not see where that smell was coming from.

"Let's climb the hill behind the spring. It's the highest point. We can see better from there."

They climbed panting and sweating up the hill. The smell of smoke grew stronger as they climbed. When they got to the top they broke through a thicket of bushes and looked south, toward the Stubbinses' farm.

"Oh, no!" Mama breathed. Her eyes were hard and bright, her lips a hard pale line. The heat pressed on Rose's forehead and the nape of her neck like hot irons. A knot tightened in the pit of her stomach.

In the distance, just beyond the Stubbinses' farm, all along the railroad tracks, billowed thick white clouds of smoke. The land was on fire!

They raced back down the hill to the house. Papa was there, unhitching the mules.

"I smell it, too," said Papa, quickly. He stared at Mama with a fierce look. "What did you see, Bess? What's burning?"

"It's the Stubbins place. He must have been burning brush and it got away from him. Oh,

Manly!" Mama cried out helplessly. "It's blowing this way!"

"Dash it all!" Papa said crossly. "Haven't we got enough on our plate as it is?" Then he began to speak sharply. "You two stay here. Fill every bucket and tub with water. Gather up all the feed sacks and soak them good. I'm going over and see if I can help. If we get separated and the fire reaches the far side of our hill . . ."

A sob jerked from Mama's throat, and she covered her face with her hands. Tears of terror flooded Rose's eyes. Papa reached out and held Mama's shoulders.

"Easy, now," he said.

"I'm sorry," Mama finally said. "It's just . . . just too much to bear thinking."

"We've all got to keep our wits," Papa said firmly. "Listen carefully, Rose. You are a big grown-up girl and you need to keep your wits as well.

"Hitch the mules to the wagon, Bess, just in case. If the fire gets close, let the stock go free. Make sure they don't run back into the barn.

They'll save themselves if you can just keep 'em out of the barn. Then drive down toward Kinnebrew's old place. Likely it'll burn itself out in the meadows, but just in case, it pays to be ready."

Then Papa saddled up May and galloped off toward the Stubbinses' farm, elbows flying up around his ears.

Now everything speeded up. Mama hitched the team. Rose ran to the barn and snatched up all the empty feed sacks. Then they hauled water from the spring. The very air seemed to tremble with their effort. Fido whined and paced back and forth in front of the house.

They poured the water from the buckets into anything they could find: the cast iron cooker, the tubs, the empty molasses barrel. All the while the smell of smoke lingered in the air.

Abe came galloping into the barnyard on one of his mules with Swiney riding on behind.

"We smelled the smoke, Missus Wilder. Where's the fire at?"

"Stubbinses' farm," Mama called out. Then they were gone.

Fire!

When all the feed sacks were soaking, they began to take things out of the house. Rose grabbed her autograph album and the quilt she was working on. There wasn't time to wrap things properly. Mama threw straw in the wagon-box, and they laid in the dishes, the bread plate that had survived the fire in South Dakota, the lamp, bedding, the clock, the books—anything they could get their hands on.

When they had got most of the small things out of the house, and the harness out of the barn, they climbed the hill again to see the fire. The smell of smoke was stronger. The blazing sun sent fingers of light poking through a thin haze.

When they got to the top, they caught their breaths. They couldn't see the flames, but thick white smoke came billowing up the hillside. The wind was stronger there, and the air was hotter.

The fire was coming, and nothing could stop it.

God's Blessing

When Mama and Rose got back down to the house, Papa was tethering May to a tree. Abe and Swiney were getting down from their mule. All their faces and hands were sooty. The mules were lathery every place the harness touched them.

"It's coming, isn't it?" Mama asked grimly.

"I'm afraid so," said Papa. "It's burned over most of the Stubbins place. He lost his barn and most of his crops.

"But we aren't licked yet! A crew of men came out from town, and they've stopped it in the field just beyond our hill. The house and barn should be safe now. But it's burning around the other side. There's still time to clear a fire-break by the orchard. If we can get it done in time, we may be able to save the trees."

More horses came galloping into the barn-yard. Men and boys jumped down and teth-ered them to trees. They carried axes and shovels. Some grabbed the sopping feed sacks; others picked up the buckets of water. Then Papa led them all past the barn, toward the orchard. Rose grabbed a feed sack and fol-lowed Mama.

When they got there, some more men were already there with axes and shovels. They were taking down the rail fence at the edge of the orchard, so it wouldn't burn up, and stack-ing the rails in the orchard.

The air rang with the sound of chopping and shouting. They were cutting trees and shrubs next to the orchard, turning the soil, trying to make the clearing bigger and longer.

The air was stifling hot now, and smoky. Rose couldn't see any fire through the trees and underbrush, but she knew it was coming.

The clearing grew and grew all afternoon, but painfully slowly. Rose didn't see how it could possibly stop the fire. Around the small apple trees there was still dry grass that would burn.

But all those men worked as though they knew what they were doing. Rose and Swiney helped drag away small cut-down trees and shrubs. They must clear the land so the fire had nothing to burn.

"You and Swiney stay in the field and beat out any sparks that fall," Mama said. They grabbed their feed sacks and waited. All around them the chopping and digging and shouting continued.

It seemed a long time that they waited. Birds darted past. Suddenly a deer bounded out of the trees right in front of Rose, running in terror with its white tail held high. Its ears were laid back, and Rose looked right into its face. It nearly knocked her over as it flew past, as if it never saw her, and disappeared into the orchard and woods beyond. Then more deer came fleeing the fire.

Finally Swiney shouted, "There it is!" Through the trees and smoke Rose caught the first glimpse of orangey-red. A tree was burning. Her stomach flip-flopped. Then several trees were burning.

The forest echoed with crackling sounds as the flames engulfed the lower limbs and then licked their way up until the whole tree was ablaze. Long fingers of flame from the treetop soared high into the air. Then burning branches broke and fell, showering sparks like logs in a fireplace.

Now Rose could feel the heat. Her face was scorching hot. Her nose burned and her eyes watered. Mama tore pieces from her apron, dunked them in water, and tied one over Rose's head and one over her own, to protect them from falling sparks.

They watched and waited as the fire burned here and there, slowly creeping toward them. Every so often little puffs of smoke rose from the grass where burning embers had been carried by the wind. Rose and Swiney took turns beating them out with their sacks. Then one of the men came with a shovel and turned the earth around that spot, to be sure all the embers were dead.

The coming fire sounded like distant wind at first. There was more crackling and popping and the hiss of wood burning. Then it began to roar, so loudly that Rose had to shout at Swiney to be heard.

The smoke thickened, blotting out the sun. It was nearly sundown now, and the flames cast an eerie yellow-orange glow over the clearing.

A gray shape scurried through the grass. "Possum!" Swiney yelled. A rabbit bounded past, and then a fat skunk waddled by.

Night began to fall as the fire finally reached the edge of the clearing. The entire woods were one scorching, roaring flame. Then someone shouted, "Watch out for snakes!"

First a few snakes, then dozens, came slithering out of the woods, parting the grass like curving ropes. Rose was very careful where she stepped in her bare feet. There were blacksnakes and even rattlesnakes. Swiney killed one with a rock, but those snakes were too frightened to stop and bite anyone, with the fire licking at their tails.

Rose dashed every which way now, pouncing on embers and beating them out with all her might. Everyone was doing it as sparks showered down on the clearing and into the orchard. Once Rose looked up as a cedar tree exploded into flames with a bang and a roar. The light of it was as bright as the sun. Then more cedar trees popped. It was terrifying, and the heat pulsed so that Rose had to turn away.

"Get back, Rose!" Mama ordered. Rose went and stood in the orchard. The leaves of the trees nearest the flames had shriveled, and the bark was hot to the touch.

The fire pressed in from the treeline. It was so hot that the men had to let it burn a little ways in the grass to get close enough to fight it. They fought it back everywhere it tried to burn through the grass, beating it down with shovels and sacks.

They fought and fought for the longest time. Then, slowly, the burning embers came less and less often. The skeletons of the cedar trees stood out against the slackening flames. The roar softened, and died away.

Suddenly Rose was blinded by a dazzling flash, then a tremendous crash. Everyone stopped, frozen in place. Lightning! No one said a word. They were all listening, straining to hear. There was a new sound, a rushing that grew louder like the roaring of a creek in flood.

Rain was coming!

A great cheer rang out all around Rose. Then she could see it, sparkling in the dying light of the fire. Thousands of little falling drops were a curtain advancing. Steadily, quickly, the rain came onward, the sound multiplied on every thirsty leaf.

It was a pattering like millions of tiny dancing feet, millions of tiny hands clapping. A cool drop struck her forehead: twenty, fifty drops splashed against her hot face. Then it came, a drenching downpour. A loud hissing rose from the smoldering woods.

Then Papa's arm was around Rose, and Mama was by his side. Rose's shoulders quivered, and he held her tight in the curve of his arm and laughed in sobbing breaths. He brushed his shirtsleeve across his eyes, red and swollen from smoke, and then got out his hand-kerchief to dab at Mama's face. But it was soaked with rain, and he laughed at himself.

"It's a good soaking rain," Papa said finally.

"Rain!" Mama cried out. "It's the blessing of God.

The Only Way to Go

Quietly and steadily the rain fell the rest of the night. They never went to bed. The excitement was too great, and there was too much to do with dawn coming. Bunting bawled to be milked, and the horses and mules and Spookendyke complained for the supper and water they had missed.

When all the animals had been cared for, they carried all their things from the wagon back into the house. The clothing and bedding were soaked, but Mama didn't mind. They had saved the house and barn and the stock. They'd lost only a few trees at the edge of the timber lot, and only one of the meadows had been burned over.

"The roof's leaking," said Rose.

"Let it leak," Mama said smiling. She set a pan under the drip that came through a warped shingle. Drop after drop made a happy tinkling sound in it.

Then, as the first gray light of dawn crept into the forest, Mama cooked eggs and salt pork for breakfast. Eggs were a treat they usually ate only on Sundays. "We've got something to celebrate," she said.

The smell of the good food cooking set Rose's stomach to growling and reminded her that they never had eaten their supper. They had been so busy fighting the fire that she had forgotten her hunger.

Rose noticed now in the light of day that Mama's and Papa's faces were red, as if they had been sunburned. And their eyebrows were partly burned off. Rose felt her own eyebrows. They were crispy.

The rain fell so evenly, so untroubled by any wind, that the doors could be thrown open.

The breath of the rain came in, sweet and damp and cool. They ate sitting on the porch, their plates in their laps, listening to the rain dripping off the roof and watching the earth drink until it could drink no more.

The hard earth became a network of little rivulets. All the leaves were drinking, all the blades of grass. Leaf dripped it to twig, twig passed it to branch, and branch to stem, and stem to root. All the dust was washed away, all the thirst and heat forgotten.

Papa said the drought was probably broken.

"We've still got an uphill climb to get through the season. Some of the corn crop might be saved," he said. "Maybe even the potatoes, although they won't be nearly so plump as last year." Mama said there would be some peas and beans, tomatoes, beets, a second planting of carrots, and turnips.

"And the orchard was saved," Rose piped.

"By the skin of our teeth and the help of all those good people," said Papa. "It was a close question, right to the end."

They talked quietly, their voices blending

with the sound of the rain. They were relaxed, refreshed, their life renewed like the life of the rejoicing fields and forest.

All the neighbors and some of the towns-people got together and helped Mr. Stubbins rebuild his barn. Papa said a train throwing sparks from its brakes had started the fire. He said Mr. Stubbins was going to get up a lawsuit against the railroad, to pay for his lost crops and barn.

Rose walked with Alva and Swiney over the burned land. To see it made Rose very sad. At the edge of the orchard where the fire had scorched the grass she found the faint trails of mice exposed. In the woods all the small trees and bushes were gone. The blackened trunks of the tall oaks and hickories stood out like ghastly skeletons with only a few naked branches left. No birds would nest there for a long time; no woods creature could make a home in such a barren place.

Yet small, valiant green leaves poked up here and there out of the ashes, miraculously finding new life in the middle of all that death. In a few weeks the whole burned-out forest was greening up with tender shoots, as if spring had come all over again.

The rest of that summer seemed almost like any other. Thunderstorms came every few days and dampened the earth enough to keep the plants growing. Weeds and new grass sprouted everywhere. But when it was nearly harvest time, the crops were late and thin.

One night at supper Papa said they must think what to do.

"There won't be any harvest to share with Stubbins," said Papa. "And we don't have enough by ourselves to last the winter and settle up the mortgage and our account at Reynolds'. Taxes are coming up, too."

"What can we do?" Mama said. "We could sell the cow, but that would take away the cream and butter money."

"Wouldn't be enough to make it worthwhile," said Papa. "Fact is, Bess, I've been talking to some folks in town and I have an idea. They need a drayman to deliver shipments from the railroad. I can also get work with Mr. Waters delivering coal oil."

"I just hate the idea of you working for somebody else again," said Mama. "I had hoped we put those days behind us once and for all. We've built the place up so well. It seems the harder we work, the farther we fall behind."

Papa twisted an end of his mustache in silence.

Mama looked at Papa with narrowed eyes. Finally she said, "There's more to it, isn't there?"

Rose got up to clear the dishes, being as quiet as she could.

"Well, I figure it this way," Papa said slowly. "Supposing we both got work in town? I mean, supposing we had two incomes for a spell?"

"But what kind of work could I possibly get? Who would take care of the stock? And the fields? And . . . What can you be thinking?" Mama said, twisting her napkin.

"I thought of all that," said Papa. "We could move to town, into the house. Abe could take over this place."

Rose gasped. She set the plates she was carrying back down on the table. Mama's mouth dropped open.

"Now just hold your tongue a minute and hear me out," Papa said. "Mrs. Cooley is fixing to move. And Mr. Waters says he might have some work for a smart gal like you, keeping his account books. We could take in boarders, and that'd give us some extra cash.

"It would just be for a year or so, until the apple trees get bigger. Then we'd move back out here with our debts all paid and ready for a fresh start."

Papa stopped talking, leaned back, and lit his pipe. Mama sat very still, looking at him but saying nothing for a long moment. Rose waited breathlessly, afraid to stir. Leaving the farm was unimaginable. Everything they had worked for, the whole reason they had come to Missouri, was right there, all around them.

Finally Mama sighed, laid her napkin on the table, smoothed it out, and folded it carefully. "I suppose you're right," she said quietly. "I don't like the idea of living in town. It's noisy, and everything we wanted is right here on the farm. But . . ." She sighed again. "Yes, I suppose we must."

"It isn't far," Papa said. "Just on the other side of the hill, not even all the way to town. We'll come out here practically every day, to help keep the place up. Abe and Swiney can take care of the mules, and do the plowing and planting. We'll take the cow and the horses and chickens with us. The house has a good backyard, room enough even for a pig."

"And Spookendyke?" Rose asked nervously. "And Fido and Blackfoot?"

"Of course," Papa said smiling. "Spookendyke and Fido, too. And Blackfoot if she wants to come. She might not like to live in town. Cats are like that."

Rose looked around the kitchen that Papa had built, where they had eaten so many meals of food they had raised with their own hands on their own land. She thought about how hard they had worked to build up the farm, fixing the house, building the barn and the henhouse, the smokehouse, all that clearing land and plowing and hoeing.

She remembered all the hardships of nature they had fought: the stony ground, the thick tree roots, the spring mud, the flood, the cyclone, the drought, the fire. She could not imagine any life different from the one they had been living. The thought of leaving it all behind, even for a little while, was too much to bear.

"Don't cry, Rose," said Mama. "Papa is right. There's only good in it for us. And you'll be nearer to Blanche, and Paul and George as well. You'll have friends to play with every day. School is just across the road. And every day you and Fido can walk Bunting and Spark out to pasture."

Then Rose thought of Alva. For two years they had tramped every inch of those hills together, playing in the creeks, hunting wild grapes, chasing rabbits, coursing bees. But ever since last fall Alva had been different toward Rose. They saw a little less of each other. Rose had her school friends, and Alva didn't like to play with them.

In truth, Rose realized, she liked Blanche a bit better than Alva. But Blanche had never been to visit at the farm. She was a town girl and didn't go visiting outside of town much. Rose began to think how pleasant it would be to see Blanche every day, and for Blanche to visit Rose any time she wished. What Mama had said was true. The more Rose thought about it, the more she warmed to the idea.

As soon as the scant harvest was in, they began to pack up the house. Mama and Rose washed all the linens and packed them in one of the trunks. They packed all but the few dishes they needed, and most of their clothing.

Then, after breakfast one crisp fall morning, Abe helped Papa drive a load of furniture to the house in town. Brown leaves fell from all the trees, and the wind kicked them up, rustling. All the rest of their belongings were stacked up on the porch.

The little house looked so empty and forlorn inside. The hollowness reminded Rose of that day so long ago when she first set foot in it. Her heart was torn. It was exciting to be moving, but at the same time she was sad to be leaving.

Papa returned, and they loaded the trunks, the dishes, the rag rugs, their winter coats, and finally the clock. For the first time since they moved in, its ticking was stilled.

Rose climbed onto the wagon seat and settled between Mama and Papa. Abe and Swiney stood in the sunny barnyard to see them off.

"Don't you worry about a thing," Abe said. "We'll care for the place as if it was our 'n."

Rose sighed mournfully as Papa chirruped to the horses. Mama put an arm around her.

"It's sad to leave, isn't it?" Mama said softly as Papa skidded the loaded wagon down the hill toward Fry Creek

Rose nodded her head. She dared not try to speak. "It's not forever," said Mama. "No matter what, we'll be coming back. But for now, this the right thing to do. Our decision is made. It doesn't do to look back. The only way to go is ahead."

Come Home to Little House

The MARTHA *Years*
By Melissa Wiley
Illustrated by Renée Graef

The CHARLOTTE *Years*
By Melissa Wiley
Illustrated by Dan Andreasen

The CAROLINE *Years*
By Maria D. Wilkes
Illustrated by Dan Andreasen

The LAURA *Years*
By Laura Ingalls Wilder
Illustrated by Garth Williams

The ROSE *Years*
By Roger Lea MacBride
Illustrated by Dan Andreasen
& David Gilleece